"There are two worlds colliding in this wonderful novel, when the Zen meditator and corporate chief executive officer in *Buddhist CEO* weaves a visual tapestry of the path toward enlightenment in the world of business. The fragrance of the incense in the silence of the zendo is as expressively depicted as the corporate tribunal where both sides of employer vs employee struggle to debate their positions. The author expresses a passion for his spiritual practice in every sentence, drawing the reader toward a discerning look at their own personal choices as they integrate compassion and mindfulness into their daily lifestyle.

"Buddhist CEO is an evocative first novel as it takes us on a narrative journey and explores the potential for synergism between the worlds of personal and business from the perspective of a mindful Zen practitioner. 5 out of 5 stars are well deserved."

—Nora D'Ecclesis, best-selling American author of *Zen Rohatsu, Multicultural Mindfulness* and *Spiritual Portals,* and winner 2022 Gold Book Award at the Los Angeles BookFest

"Thane has written an extraordinary book in *The Buddhist CEO*. He identifies that the foundation of being a great CEO is based on showing gratitude, compassion, peace, love, and honesty. Thane's book highlights the huge challenge that gets in the way of CEO's leading with these attributes—our ego. Using Thane's brilliant storytelling skills, his book is a blueprint to be a different type of CEO—*The Buddhist CEO*. I recommend that all CEO's should take the time to read it."

—Neil Francis, chairman and author of *The Creative Thinking Book, Positive Thinking* and *The Entrepreneur's Book*

"*The Buddhist CEO* by Thane Lawrie is a beautiful story melding Zen practice with the role of a CEO in a large non-profit social service organization. Lawrie writes with an authenticity that clearly comes from his own direct experience, and in lovely ways intermingles moving human exchanges, daily challenges of organizational work life, and the influence that a regular and committed Zen practice can have on these. I particularly liked the thoughtful account of Zen retreats, finding them to be a wonderful reminder of what one can experience when one enters extended silence with a group of engaged practitioners. I highly recommend this book to anyone with an interest in spiritual practice, and a need to make one's way with balance and grace through the daily ups and downs of our modern, active lives."

—Christopher Keevil, Zen Teacher, author of *Finding Zen in the Ordinary*, and founder of Wellspring Consulting, serving leaders of non-profit organizations

"A compelling story reminding me of my own struggles with difficult events in life, and how Buddhism gave me a way to see all of that very differently."

—Thomas Wharton, author of *Ice Fields*

"Thane Lawrie's debut novel is tightly drawn, sometimes amusing, always profound, evocative, and universally reflective. Balancing the tensions between the demands of a highly pressured profession and the constant quest for spiritual enlightenment and peace, Lawrie paints a vivid portrait of the inner workings of a modern man striving to honour the gentility of his beliefs while confronting the challenges and frustrations of leadership. A splendid and thoughtful revelation, Lawrie's work quietly opens the door on the questions we all carry in our deepest core. This is a book to be read slowly, savored, and absorbed."

—Greg Fields, author *Through the Waters and the Wild*, 2022 Winner, Independent Press Award for Literary Fiction

"A prescient read for everybody: religious aspirants, committed business leaders, and for all who consistently 'overdo it' in life. Read slowly as you would a sutra. It is said the Buddhist scriptures (a poetic form of conveying universal truths born of direct experience) were written at 'deaths door,' that is, having had one's faith extremely and severely tested in adversity unimaginable and lived to pass on digested truth. What greater gift could there be.

"In the face of a life limiting illness (FND), Hamish, a dedicated Buddhist practitioner, is forced to change his lifestyle. What truths does he derive from entering the fires of suffering and come out the other side? Perhaps, for starters, labels have to drop away? No Buddhist, no CEO."

—Reverend Master Mugo White, Throssel Hole Buddhist Abbey

"In his work, Lawrie sheds light to a commonly unseen, but very dangerous problem: the rising frequency of functional illnesses across highly demanding professions. With vividly moving scenes, we travel through Hamish's life's journey; going from a remarkably functioning individual to falling ill, witnessing firsthand the struggles of people with Functional Neurological Disorders (FND), and how Buddhism and spirituality are vital tools in the quest of managing these conditions. A must read for every working professional!"

—Dr. Yadira Velazquez, MD, Neurologist and Clinical Neurophysiologist, Science and Shamanism International

"Thane Lawrie's book, *The Buddhist CEO*, is a rare exploration of a career in management within a people-centred charity. It balances both the objective workings of the organisation with the personal and spiritual life of its CEO. It covers the very human story of what happens when good managerial intentions meet at times with some underhanded and divisive staff behaviour. Thane tracks for us the highs and lows around taking responsibility and making the hard choices that his role demands, and the price to be paid in terms of personal stress in maintaining your integrity. The book becomes quite a dramatic page turner as we travel with the author, through the complexities of this human story. The overall effect of the book is to give us an honest and even uplifting insight into the human world of managing an organisation, where the very ups and downs becomes the fuel for going deeper in our own spiritual journey."

—Reverend Master Favian Straughan, Prior of Portobello
Buddhist Priory

"Each of us, whether consciously or not, is simply trying to live what the Buddhists call 'this precious human life,' as best we can. Many of us reach for the literalism of nonfiction works and/or the symbolism of fiction to guide us. This novel is unlikely to be like anything you have read before. It's not every day you get to read a book where Buddhist protagonists and workplace antagonists duke it out within the same pages.

"The late great Joseph Campbell, professor of literature, would probably have agreed that Hamish, the lead character in *The Buddhist CEO*, is essentially following the arc of the 'hero's journey' that Campbell is famed for popularising. But this is only part of the book's appeal. Editors and agents endlessly advise authors to 'write what you know.' In every sentence, paragraph and chapter, the author has done precisely that. Like all things Buddhist, experience happens on many levels. This book is no exception.

"On one level, you will get to enjoy a fictional story with interesting settings, conflicts and contrasts (something else authors are encouraged to do). On another, you get to relive and learn from the true life trials the author has had to survive in order to put before you the book you now hold in your hands.

"Delve in and enjoy."

—Matt Jardine, author of *The Buddhist Millionaire &*
The Hardest Path

"A fascinating exploration of two converging worlds. Author Thane Lawrie guides us through a captivating story of highs and lows–the realization of his (and our) own humanness as the challenges of executive leadership and life with a neurological condition become part of his spiritual journey. A book that is sure to transform, it's a must-read throughout our own personal exploration to live our lives fully and manage the complexities of daily life."

—Ryan Lindner, author of *The Half-Known Life: What Matters Most When You Are Running Out of Time*

"A compelling read pertinent for all of us striving to do and be our best in a complex, often overly demanding world. Drawn in by Lawrie's storytelling and his commitment to seeking higher ground and the elusive state of balance and peace, here's a book to share with friends and colleagues alike."

—Dr. Amy Rothenberg, author of *You Finished Treatment, Now What? A Field Guide for Cancer Survivors*

"Whether or not you're a Buddhist or a CEO, you'll recognize in Lawrie's tale of battling the 'shoulds' of conventional and spiritual life and how the body invariably tells a truth of its own."

—Ginny Whitelaw Roshi, author of *Resonate* and *The Zen Leader*

"As Lawrie initially transports the reader from the spiritual environment to the 'real world' the contrast is easily understood. For his character, Hamish, life presents personal challenges, mentally, physically, and spiritually, as he deeply navigates his own fragilities. *The Buddhist CEO* struggles with the how's and why's of others' actions and work challenges, as he strives not to take them personally and to be empathetic, even with those who hurt others or misrepresent the truth. Clinging to Buddhist transcendental meditation for reprieve, Hamish asks, 'How long will this feeling of peace last?' And as work issues evolve, he contends with circumstances while adhering to Buddhist beliefs."

—Jan Moberg, author of *Chaplain's Walk: The Spiritual Side of Medicine*

The Buddhist CEO

Thane Lawrie

ISBN 978-1-64663-856-7

Published by

 köehlerbooks™

3705 Shore Drive
Virginia Beach, VA 23455
800-435-4811
www.koehlerbooks.com

THE
BUDDHIST
CEO

THANE LAWRIE

VIRGINIA BEACH
CAPE CHARLES

I dedicate this book to all beings,
human and nonhuman,
seeking to live an enlightened life.

Follow Thane at Thanelawrie.com or on Twitter @BuddhistCEO

TABLE OF CONTENTS

CHAPTER 1

The Monastery—My Second Home

THE BODHISATTVA PRECEPTS

Refrain from killing

Refrain from stealing

Refrain from sexual misconduct

Refrain from saying that which is untrue

Refrain from indulging intoxicants

Refrain from speaking about others

Refrain from being proud of yourself
and devaluing others

Refrain from being mean with either
Dharma or wealth

Refrain from indulging anger

Refrain from defaming the Three Treasures

The *ting* of the bell signaled the end of our meditation. A line of Buddhist trainees on either side of the Zendo bowed in unison, as did Reverend Lucas, the monk leading our weeklong retreat. We all stood, and the line of trainees on either side of the Zendo turned to face each other, hands held in *gassho*, and bowed. The deep silence was broken only by the creaking bones of the trainees' legs. I felt a slight sense of relief that the week's final period of meditation was over. We had been sitting for at least ten periods of thirty-five minutes each day. Although this is extremely liberating, it certainly takes its toll on the body. But the insights it brings is always worth it.

Reverend Lucas spoke to us all. "Well, quite a week."

We all smiled and laughed in appreciation. I am sure every trainee faced their own demons as we sat facing the wall that week, but with it came a deep sense of appreciation for each other, for Reverend Lucas, and for all the monks living in this incredible place. Sitting in a Zen monastery in meditation for most of the week whilst observing silence is an incredible experience, but I would not describe it as easy.

Reverend Lucas continued, "This is the end of the retreat, the end of this weeklong *sesshin*. Thanks for coming and sharing your practice with me and others. I've learned lots from you all. I'm sure you have all faced difficulties—sore backs, sore knees, feeling tired and irritated with lack of sleep or recurring thoughts about what awaits you out there in the world. However, I hope you've all felt a deepening of your practice. Remember that practice doesn't begin and end when you arrive and leave the monastery. Training goes on and is possible in every aspect of our lives, wherever we find ourselves. Home life, work life, social life, sangha life, and family life. This peace, this sense of clarity, and this sense of feeling grounded is always available to us. It might be harder to see or experience when you are caught up in the outside world, but as we discussed, try to bring a bit of what you learned this week into your daily routine.

"You won't be able to meditate ten times a day when you're back with your families and back at work," he continued. "Remember, though, that we monks only meditate that often at certain times of the year. Try to commit to meditating in the morning and once in the evening if possible. Read one of the short scriptures each day, and try to live by the precepts as best you can. Never beat yourself up if you stray slightly or miss a day. Compassion is the key. Compassion towards other beings, but do remember to show compassion towards yourself, and as I said during the week, it's so easy to be compassionate to others and forget to be compassionate to ourselves. There is a light lunch prepared for you downstairs in the dining hall. Please have a safe and pleasant journey home."

Reverend Lucas then held his hands in gassho and directed a smile at us all—a smile that seemed to come from a different place and penetrated one's being with its sincerity. We all smiled back, hands in gassho, and bowed respectfully as this inspiring monk walked gracefully from the Zendo.

After a light lunch I stood on the steps of the monastery and soaked in the peace one last time before heading back into the world. *What a setting*, I thought: Throssel Hole Buddhist Abbey, perched high in the Pennine Hills in Northern England amongst trees planted by the monks, which extend to the edge of the monastery grounds. Beyond the trees, desolate moorland extends over rugged hills. Yet these rolling hills possess a timeless beauty. At times, the monastery seems to hover above the world on its own celestial plane, cloaked in a silence pierced only by birdsong.

The monastery comprises a series of buildings. On the west side of the grounds is a large two-story structure—the monks' quarters, consisting of the monks' bedrooms, their own washing facilities, small offices, and large library. Laypeople do not often visit these more private areas. A short walk along a track offering stunning views over the rolling Pennine Hills leads to a complex of three 2-story buildings—two meditation halls and a structure housing the kitchen, lay common room, and laypeople accommodation—and a house.

The meditation halls, one for the monks and one dedicated to laypeople like me, are large, but in true Zen tradition, they are plain except for the altar. The laypeople's meditation hall is on the first floor, and at the east end, set in beautiful sandstone, is a huge arched window which is twenty feet high and ten feet wide. I love looking out of this window. When we practice walking meditation, we are meant to concentrate on our walking, but I cannot help sneaking little glances through the window every time I pass. The window overlooks a mixture of deciduous trees and firs in the monastery grounds, and then past those to the hills nearby.

These hills are often cloaked in mist, adding to the timeless quality of this place. *How long have I been here? Is it three days or three weeks?* I often wonder. It is a world apart from my chief executive life back home.

The north and south walls of the hall have compartments colored the same light green as the walls, and so barely visible, and adorned with a delicate golden tree. The compartments are common in Zen Buddhist temples. Within them is stored a mattress and pillow for sleeping. Above each compartment is another for storing your belongings, such as your travel bag, clothes, and toiletries.

Traditionally in Zen monasteries, as is the case here, Buddhist trainees sleep in the meditation hall at night. A curtain is drawn after the last period of meditation in the evening. Women sleep on one side of the curtain and men on the other.

At the west end of the hall is a beautiful altar bearing a large Buddha statue, gold and about six feet in height. The Buddha sits in meditation, looking down at us. This image has always fascinated me, even as a child. There is a gracefulness about the Buddha, a sense of peace, tranquility, and purpose—qualities I have longed to experience and develop in my own life.

The statue is surrounded by offerings of fruit laid out on colored dishes and interspersed with several candles. The altar is beautifully illuminated by ornate lights from above. At night, some of these remain lit, and I have found myself gazing at the Buddha statue for several hours before I finally fall asleep. The meditation hall is carpeted with a thick, light-orange carpet. I'm always thankful for its thickness, which provides relief when my knees start to ache after long meditation.

This is my spiritual home—the place where I come to escape the world, recharge my Buddhist practice, and energize my life. Here is a chance to practice deeply without interruption and to converse with the monks who live and run this precious place, and seek their view and advice on life's dilemmas. Buddhist practitioners aim to avoid clinging to thoughts, places, and things. It sometimes seems ironic to me, as someone attempting to practice the Buddhist path by letting go of my attachments, that I feel so damned attached to this place.

My wife says that she has rarely seen me cry, but I cry every time I leave the monastery.

"What does it do to you?" she asks.

"A good question," I respond.

What *does* it do to me? I think it is a mixture of the beautiful surroundings, embedded in nature, the haunting cry of tawny owls as darkness falls, the long periods of meditation, the sincerity of practice shown by the monks and the other laypeople on retreat. All this just blows me open. It strips away my ego, this thin film of ideas that supposedly makes up who I am. When I get down to the bare bones of it, there's not much there at all. The deep stillness of this place reveals something that can't be explained easily in words. What I find on retreat in a monastery when the world has dropped away is a deep peace, a contentment, a knowing that everything is okay in this moment.

The peace of the monastery is a strange contrast to my life at home. Back in the world, I'm a chief executive officer, the CEO of a large charity called Rural Cancer Care (RCC). I am lucky to have this job; it provides a good salary, and because of it, my family can afford to live a little. I enjoy the benefits, but on reflection I wonder if the happiest I've ever been was when money was short, my wife and I were younger, and the kids were barely knee high.

There's no doubt that some of the most special moments in my life, where I have felt a bond with people like no other, have been on Buddhist retreat. It's incredible just how connected I feel to others here. This seems counterintuitive. Surely if I'm on a silent retreat, there is no opportunity to bond. But I find it's quite the opposite, and I get a sense that others on retreat feel the same way. There's something about gently working with other people, supporting each other, no ridicule, no sense of competing against one another, just working together in an almost rhythmic fashion and showing gratitude for each other's efforts. If anyone makes a mistake, they are met with compassion.

The most striking illustration I have of this feeling happened on a retreat I attended many years ago, an important ceremony within the Soto Zen Buddhist tradition called *jukai*. This is a weeklong ceremony and retreat for laypeople to commit to live by and practice the ten Bodhisattva precepts and, in so doing, to formally become a Buddhist. When I attended this retreat in 2003, one of the women participating had to leave early in the morning on the final day. She lived in Cornwall, which is in the far south of England and about as far from Throssel as it is possible to be in the United Kingdom. To make it home that day, she had to catch an early train, so she left just after breakfast.

On retreat, everyone eats their meals communally and in silence, but after we all finished our breakfast, she stood and said, "Can I just interrupt you all before my long journey home to say how much I've enjoyed being with you all this week?" Her voice broke. "I can honestly say I've never felt so close to a group of human beings in all my life." Tears flowed freely down her kind face as she struggled to say, "Thank you all so much, and I wish you all so much happiness for your future."

We all beamed back at her, our hands held in gassho as she left the room, wiping tears from her cheeks. I know well the sense of connection she felt that day, and I think of her heartfelt sincerity often. In the media I'm aware of the plethora of advice in newspapers, online, and in television programs, discussing our psychology and how to be well. Rarely do they mention the benefits of silence and working with others compassionately and mindfully. It's a shame that few people in the modern world ever get a chance to experience this depth of being and the sense of connection that comes with it.

As I stood on the monastery stairs, I took some deep breaths and soaked in the atmosphere of the place. I smiled to myself and thought, *How long will this feeling of deep peace last?* Experience has taught me that it will last a few days but will slowly diminish once back in my worldly life, though it won't disappear altogether.

I had a nice, long drive home to look forward to—over the Pennine Hills and then into Scotland before driving up the east coast to my home in rural Aberdeenshire—and the sun was shining. I planned to stop along the way to take in the scenery. Every good road trip needs a few coffee and cake stops along the way.

I was about to deal with a very tricky situation at work. Standing in a monastic setting made the situation more surreal. Here I was, the committed Zen Buddhist who for many years had been content attempting to live the Buddhist life. Simple, peaceful, grateful, contemplative, diligent, honest, compassionate, non-clinging, and not particularly career ambitious.

However, I had found that I was good at some things. I seemed to naturally get on with people, manage and run things well, motivate people, make good decisions. Career opportunities opened up for me as my life progressed, culminating in becoming the CEO of a fantastic organization, RCC, at the age of forty-three.

All had gone well in the first three years of my CEO journey, but then I started to experience strange and challenging behaviors from staff, and it made me question myself as a Buddhist and a CEO. How did someone without much ambition become a CEO? Was this the right path for me to take? At times I had to dismiss people from their duties, discipline staff, and make tough decisions that made me unpopular. Buddhist teaching is all about letting go, living in the moment, and cultivating a life of compassion and peace. *Is this compatible with being a CEO?* These thoughts would race through my head from time to time. In true Zen fashion, I tried to observe them and not get too caught up in them. But this is easier said than done, especially given the road I had traveled.

I had married at twenty-two and had two kids by the time I was twenty-four, so it was difficult to turn down opportunities that meant having more money for the family. I deeply love my wife and boys, but our journey has not always been easy. I met Beth when we were students at Aberdeen University. I was studying social work and management, and she nursing. I fell in love with this amazing woman immediately. Thankfully, Beth felt the same way about me! We moved in together quickly, renting a one-bedroom flat near the beach in Aberdeen, and our boys arrived just after we graduated. For some time, money was tight, but we were happy sleeping on a pull-down sofa in the living room whilst our boys shared the one bedroom together.

I look back at the early years of our family life with fondness. In one sense they were difficult times, mainly due to the fact we had little money, but we lived well and were happy. I had been interested in Zen Buddhism for a few years before meeting Beth, and after meeting her, I joined a local Soto Zen group in Aberdeen. The group was affiliated to the Order of Buddhist Contemplatives (OBC), a monastic order founded by the late Reverend Master Jiyu Kennet. This amazing Zen monk was one of the first Westerners, and the first woman, to be accepted into monastic life in Japan in the early 1960s. Once her Zen master, Keido Chisan, certified Reverend Jiyu as a Zen master, he asked her to come to the West and establish an order that would welcome and encourage Buddhist practice amongst laypeople, and provide opportunities for those interested in monastic life. She founded the OBC and established two large training monasteries, one of which was Throssel Hole.

As I slowly walked towards my car parked in the monastery grounds, I felt childlike, reluctant to leave, dragging my feet, my gut wrenching at the thought of tearing myself away from my spiritual home. I caught sight of Reverend Lucas, his brown robes flapping slightly in the gentle breeze. I raised my hands in gassho, and this quiet monk beamed a timeless smile at me and raised his hands in gassho too. This smile said more to me than many words.

"Ah, Hamish, nice to see you before you leave. Have you enjoyed your stay with us?"

"I most certainly have, Reverend. I most certainly have."

We talked briefly, and he referred to our discussion earlier that week about what I was heading back to at work. He reminded me again to stay grounded in the practice, act with a pure heart, and do what I felt was the right thing. "Check and be sure your actions are in line with the Buddhist precepts." I thanked him, said my goodbyes, and slowly drove out of the monastery grounds, a tear in my eye and a heart full of gratitude.

CHAPTER 2

Elaine

> For more than seventy years, I have been
> making Myself dizzy observing men.
>
> I have abandoned trying to penetrate
> men's good and bad actions.
>
> Coming and going is a sign of weakness.
>
> Heavy snow in the dead of night—
>
> Under the weather-beaten window,
> one incense stick.
>
> —*Ryokan*

Two weeks prior to my trip to the monastery, I found myself in an odd and troubling situation at work. I had Jim, our IT executive, join me in my office and then asked him to take a seat.

"Unfortunately, Jim, we might have a security breach on our hands."

"Oh dear, what's up?" he said.

"We've been here before, but I just need to remind you that this conversation is in strict confidence because if my hunch is correct, what I am about to tell you could result in someone being suspended from the company. I'm hoping you can help me get to the bottom of this. I'll explain briefly what's happened and how you can help me.

"Last week we held a Staffing and Resources Committee meeting to discuss possible changes to the working patterns and remuneration of a senior member of staff, Jason. Obviously, the outcome of that meeting is sensitive and private, and the content of the meeting should have remained confidential. In attendance at the meeting were three board members, including our chairman, and me. I know that none of those guys have said anything to anyone about the outcome of the meeting. However, information discussed at that meeting has been divulged to Jason by someone not present at the meeting, and it's caused bad feeling between us. I need to find out how on earth this happened."

Jason, my partnership and sustainability manager, had approached me the week before to tell me he was struggling. He had four young kids and his parents were unwell. They normally helped a lot with the kids and now, due to poor health, weren't able to. This put more pressure on Jason and his wife and meant he was supporting his parents as often as he could. The mixture of work pressure and family life had begun to take its toll.

Jason was in his late thirties. He was a proud man who was widely respected across the company. I knew it had taken a lot for him to raise this issue with me, and I wanted to help. We talked through how I could offer him support, and we agreed that he would work three days a week instead of five for the next few weeks. We would review the situation monthly. I offered to keep him on full pay as he had a family to support. I know how this feels, and besides, Jason had been loyal to RCC for many years, so I was keen to help him during this difficult time.

If a senior member of staff was dropping their hours significantly, it had to be approved by the board. We had a sub-group of the board, called our Staffing and Resources Committee, that ratified these decisions. I told Jason I would convene a meeting of the committee the next week, and I was hopeful that the board would support this arrangement. Jason was appreciative, but he asked for this to go no further than me and the relevant members of the committee. I assured him that this would be dealt with in the strictest of confidence. The Staffing and Resources Committee discussed the issue on Friday and agreed to support Jason's request in light of his commitment and long service to RCC.

In the last hour, Jason had asked for a word with me. I knew something was up just by the look on his face. He told me that Elaine, one of our service managers, had approached him that afternoon and asked if he was okay. Jason thought this was a slightly odd question but said, "I'm fine. Why wouldn't I be?" Elaine said she'd heard he'd been depressed, which infuriated Jason.

I told the relevant parts of this story to Jim, but the question now was how Elaine knew about this. I had honored Jason's request to keep the reasons behind his request private, and it now looked like I had not kept my word. I hoped Jim would be able to help.

"Jim, I wonder, can we find out who has accessed this information by looking at our IT? I need you to check if anyone searched for the report that I submitted to that meeting on Friday."

"Where did you save this document, Hamish?" asked Jim.

"I saved it in the leadership drive, then in the HR folder, and then in a folder called Staff Reports."

"Sounds like someone has been doing some snooping around," said Jim. "Let's see what we can find for you. Not many people have access to the leadership drive, though. In fact, only the leadership team have full access to the folder, which makes this very worrying. Let me run a search and see if anyone has accessed this file of late."

He stared at the screen as the computer did its work, and his demeanor changed quickly from his usual happy, relaxed look to one of surprise. "Whoa, my God, Hamish; I did not expect this at all." Jim turned the computer screen round so I could see it. There was a small box in the middle of the screen, and two names appeared: my name and Elaine's!

"Elaine," I said out loud. "I did not expect that either. Bloody hell, Jim. I can't understand how she's managed to access this."

I was shocked because Elaine had worked for the company for about eight years. She could be negative at times and seemed to lack vision, but I trusted her and recognized that she was hardworking. I never suspected she was capable of this.

"Can I just be clear, Jim? Does this mean that the only two people to access this file are Elaine and myself?"

"Exactly right," said Jim. He continued, "Okay, let's see what she did with this file. Did she save it or send it to anyone, I wonder."

He had regained his normal calm look, but it soon changed again, this time to shock. "Christ, Hamish, take a look at this. I can't bloody believe what I'm seeing here." Jim turned the computer so I could read it.

The search showed that Elaine had saved the file into a folder on her desktop. She'd named the folder DEFCOM1. And it contained other files. Jim and I stared at each other, incredulous and silent for a long while.

Things like this are not supposed to happen in our company. We are a charity supporting people in northern Scotland who are living with cancer. Our services help those in rural areas who need to travel to hospitals in the cities of Aberdeen, Dundee, or Inverness for daily cancer treatment. The treatment is usually offered on an outpatient basis, but these people struggle to access the care they need. At RCC we offer comfortable accommodation and support during treatment. We drive patients to their appointments and back again, and whilst staying with us they can access all kinds of support, like massage, counseling, and complementary therapies, and daily entertainment to keep them occupied, comfortable, and active. We also offer rooms to people living rurally who want to support a loved one whilst they're in hospital but who perhaps can't afford to pay for hotels.

As a company, we don't have much money, but we have compassionate, highly motivated staff. This type of work really fits with my Buddhist ideals. I can't think of a better job than to support fellow human beings at a time of great need and to lead an organization like this, which genuinely seeks to treat its staff well and make a difference in our customers' lives.

But this situation wasn't the first I'd had to deal with of late. It made me wonder if this was really what I wanted to do with my life.

I asked Jim to look at the DEFCOM1 folder and explain what was in it and how on earth Elaine managed to access the leadership folder when she wasn't a member of the leadership team. In the folder was the report that I had presented to the Staffing and Resources Committee outlining Jason's situation, and, alarmingly, an occupational health report relating to another member of staff. There were also several company policies, such as "Fairness at Work" and "Equality and Diversity." These policies were available to all staff, and it seemed odd that they were included in this folder.

Jim noticed something else—an icon at the bottom of the screen that looked like a small microphone. He had never seen that before on any of our company laptops, and it made him suspicious. He then noticed a subfolder labeled *Secret*. Inside was a list of about fifty documents with various names and numbers beside them.

My name featured a lot, but so did the names of other members of my senior management team: Steven, Jason, Sheena, and Leona. I found this information hard to take in.

"My God, Jim, what on earth are these files?"

"I'm not sure, Hamish; there's only one way to find out," he said. Jim clicked on the first file, which was named Hamish1. There was silence, then a sound; it was an audio recording. Jim turned up the volume so we could hear what was being said.

I could not believe my ears. This was a recording that Elaine had secretly made of a conversation we'd had several weeks ago. My mind reeled and I mentally grappled with what I was hearing and seeing on Elaine's laptop. Anger and disgust welled up at the violation. I had trusted Elaine implicitly, considered her a good colleague. But she'd made secret recordings of our conversations and had been snooping around our IT system, looking at documents she was not authorized to access. I was lost for words. I could tell Jim was as well. Jim and Elaine got on well and sat close to each other in the office.

Jim clicked on the other files, and it became clear that these were all secret recordings, likely made without people's permission. Other documents were related to company passwords, but thankfully these were encrypted. But why save them? It didn't look good.

"Okay, so how did she do it? How on earth did she access these files in the leadership drive?" I asked. Jim looked confused and checked to see if she was on the permissions list for this folder. There was her name. "Could she have added herself to these permissions, Jim?"

Jim rubbed his chin thoughtfully with his hand. "To be honest, Hamish, it's only me who can authorize this action after it's been approved by you. But why would I have given her permission? And I would've asked you first."

After a moment he said, "Do you remember a few months back, Elaine was working on some sensitive HR issues involving a couple of members of her team? You asked me to temporarily grant her access to the leadership drive for the duration of that piece of work. I'm sorry, Hamish, but it looks like I never took her off again."

Though slightly annoyed with Jim, I recognized that I had played my part in this as well. I could have checked to make sure her access had been revoked once she'd completed the task she was working on. Clearly, we needed a procedure that installed a review or end date on special permissions. This wasn't the time to dwell on this issue, but I was glad that we now understood how she'd accessed these files.

I told Jim I needed time to think about my next actions and would consult our human resources manager. Thanking him for his assistance, I reminded him again that this had to remain confidential and asked him not to disable Elaine's access to the leadership drive just yet; I wanted to think this through before letting on that we'd discovered this information.

I sat motionless for a while, taking in the gravity of what had just happened. I glanced around my office. The room was fairly small, but it had two windows with a great view over the River Dee, and I rose to stare out of one of them now, watching the river slowly snake towards the sea. Mist covered the water's surface like a silver blanket, capped by a deep-blue sky broken by the occasional cloud. Geese flew across the blue backdrop. As I followed my breath, I felt my chest rise and fall slowly. I drew upon my Buddhist training and the teachings I had followed for more than twenty-five years to ground myself in the moment and bring clarity and peace to the unfolding events.

My mind settled a little after the shock. I tried to not indulge or add to my racing emotions and thoughts but simply be aware of and watch them. I sensed disbelief, shock, and anger. How could Elaine have done this? Judgment crept in quickly. *What an absolute scoundrel!* I thought. *How dare she act in this way.* I was also perplexed. *How could she do this to herself and her partner?* Elaine was quite young, thirty-three, and she lived with her partner, Anna. They had lived together for years but only recently announced they were a couple and intended to marry soon. Elaine had told me and her colleagues they hoped to adopt a child of their own.

Surely she must have known there would be ramifications for her job if she were caught. Could she not see that I was a good guy with no malice towards her? But Buddhist training had taught me that these thoughts were just my ego trying to rationalize the situation. I also knew that none of this was helpful.

As I stared out of my office window, a thought occurred to me. Recently our general manager, Steven, who directly line managed Elaine, had left the company quickly. Elaine had made it clear that she expected to be promoted. Because Steven left quickly and unexpectedly, I chose to promote someone else to the post on a temporary basis. This post was too important to potentially leave vacant for a couple of months or more whilst it was advertised externally, and Elaine wasn't the right person for the job.

I promoted another of my managers, Bill Smith. A furious Elaine confronted me at the time. I didn't mind this as such, as I believed it was only fair to give her an explanation. Although it was a difficult conversation, I told Elaine that I rated her highly and believed that she was hardworking and genuinely cared about delivering a world-class service to our RCC customers. However, I explained that I sometimes experienced her as negative. She could get bogged down in detail at times, and I felt this really held her back. On one occasion, Elaine had been reluctant to take on a piece of work I asked her to do. She ultimately took on the work, but this left a niggling doubt as to whether I wanted her on my leadership team if I couldn't count on her standing by my side when I needed her.

These were all things that she could work on, and I was willing to mentor her in this regard. I made clear that the job would be advertised, and she had every right to apply.

Was this it? Had Elaine become resentful towards me and the company? My mind spun with confusion. Below, an elderly couple carried their shopping up the street, and a silver car drove past the office. These everyday things brought me back to the moment and helped clear my mind.

I could speculate all I wanted about Elaine's motives, but whatever they were, I had to act. What she had done was serious and warranted immediate suspension until the situation could be fully investigated. I discussed the process with our HR manager, Morag, and she agreed that my intended actions were appropriate under the circumstances. Morag helped me compose a letter detailing the reasons for Elaine's suspension and what would happen next.

I phoned Elaine at her desk, but there was no reply. I walked through the office to find her. She was just returning to her desk with a steaming cup of coffee and a chocolate biscuit. Other staff were nearby, so I acted calmly to avoid making a scene or embarrassing her in front of others. It struck me as odd that I was worried about her feelings when I felt so violated by her actions towards me and her colleagues. As she sat at her desk, I said as casually as I could, "Elaine, could I have a quick word with you up in my office please?"

"No problem, I'll be up in two minutes," she replied.

I made my way upstairs and sat in my chair with only the letter in front of me on my desk. I'd instructed Jim to disable Elaine's access to her computer and all our IT systems as soon as she left her station. I was aware of feeling tense. I focused on my breathing, and an image of the Buddha came to my mind. I needed to be firm and factual. Although I was angry, I had to act as compassionately as I could.

"Take a seat, Elaine," I said as she entered the room a few minutes later.

"Everything okay, Hamish?" At this moment I sensed that she'd detected something wasn't quite right.

"Unfortunately, Elaine, everything is not okay. I'll come straight to the point. I'm suspending you from your duties as I've reason to suspect that you've accessed files that you weren't authorized to access, and that you shared the information within these documents with another member of staff. I also have reason to suspect that you secretly recorded conversations between us and conversations between you and other members of the leadership team. It's also likely that you've downloaded an occupational health report relating to another member of staff.

"You'll be suspended on full pay until a thorough investigation is carried out. The investigation will be conducted as quickly as possible, and you will be interviewed as part of the process. The investigation will decide if there's evidence of wrongdoing on your part, and the findings could recommend that you have nothing to answer for or that this matter should lead to disciplinary procedures. This letter explains what I've said to you just now and details what will happen next. I now have to ask you to give me your office keys, staff ID badge, laptop, and your work mobile phone."

I watched Elaine's expression as I spoke to her. She didn't look surprised, and I suspected that she knew this was coming. She must have known that Jason was going to raise this with me and that I would have to take some sort of action. Strangely, the only time any emotion registered on her face was when I said that she had to return her phone.

"Wow, Hamish, I wasn't expecting that. All I can say is that I don't know anything about this, and I can assure you that I'm innocent." She paused. "You said I have to return my work phone?"

"Yes, that's correct," I replied. "It will potentially be looked at as part of the investigation."

"That might be a problem, Hamish. I don't have a personal phone, so how will you be able to stay in touch with me?"

I found this a very odd response to what I'd just told her and wondered what was on that phone that she didn't want me to see. More secret recordings? "Sorry, Elaine. I need you to hand over all of your work-related equipment to me."

Elaine reluctantly handed me her phone. She was now ready to argue her case and ask questions, but I made it clear that this was not the time for questions nor arguments. She would be given every opportunity to state her case during the investigation.

The situation was awkward and the room full of tension. I thought of the Bodhisattva precepts and my commitment to following them. *Is this compassionate action?* I wondered. *Is suspending someone with the real potential of disciplinary action compatible with my Buddhist practice? All I really want is to live life peacefully and show compassion towards my fellow beings.* These thoughts jolted me back into the moment. I still felt the tension, but I sensed that compassion could find a place here.

"Elaine, I realize this is a shock for you. I'm sure that you don't want to draw attention to yourself when we walk back into the office. I want to make this as dignified as possible. I'll walk down to the office with you where I'll give you a couple of minutes to collect any possessions from your desk. I'll not be far from you, and I would ask that you leave quietly and professionally and let the investigation run its course over the coming days, when you'll be given your chance to tell your side of the story." This seemed to ease the friction slightly, and we made our way downstairs to the main office.

Elaine went to her desk as I watched from nearby. She collected a few things and headed for the corridor leading out of the building. I walked slowly behind her in a way that I hoped didn't make it obvious to other staff that something was up. She left the building, got into her car, and drove off.

It was now late in the afternoon, and I felt drained. I've studied, attended conferences, and read literature on leadership and heard many great leaders give talks about their leadership journeys and how they have coped with the pressures of their roles. Many of the leaders I've admired have said that on a human level, they never enjoyed dealing with these types of situations. I certainly didn't feel at this moment like some heroic CEO impervious to pressure and strain. I went to the bathroom, and in the mirror, I looked drawn; my face was white.

The Buddha taught that there is no self, an idea that runs contrary to how we in the West often view ourselves. The Buddhist view is that through meditation and mindfulness, we can touch upon our Buddha nature, which is characterized by a sense of feeling grounded, compassionate, content, and at ease. We are taught to see our thoughts and feelings like passing clouds in the sky. Sometimes we might feel peaceful, and at other times we might feel anger, joy, disappointment, or any other human emotion. The Buddhist view is to not get caught up in these feelings or thoughts. We are taught to gently bring ourselves back to the present moment and let these thoughts and feelings drift by, or to let them be there if they're persistent but to try not to identify with them.

As I considered this and tried to put these teachings into practice, I walked back into my office and sat for a moment. What struck me was how hurt I felt. Despite years of Buddhist training, I still felt this strong sense of "I": *I* had been wronged, *I* had been cheated, *I* had been hurt, *I* had been threatened, *I* had been set up by Elaine. Then: *How could Elaine have done this to me? Me, a Buddhist whose only intention is to help other beings! Me, who has only ever tried to support Elaine in her career and to help her develop as a professional. Me, who despite being annoyed by Elaine's lack of drive and her negativity still offers friendly advice and support.*

This pattern of thinking was not helpful, but I had to let it do its thing. My mind latched onto all sorts of theories about Elaine. Years of study and professional training in social work had taught me how people who were not fortunate enough to have been born into a loving and supportive family can struggle in life; a loving and supportive family who meets your emotional needs are the cornerstone to developing a well-balanced personality. Those not born into such a situation can have difficulties forming positive relationships with people. Was this why Elaine had acted this way?

Elaine was an open person and talked frequently about her upbringing. She'd been brought up in Wales and only moved to Scotland as an adult. Her childhood had been tough, and she was one of four siblings, including a brother and two sisters. Her dad left the family home when she was young. Her mum had done the best she could but struggled financially and suffered from frequent bouts of depression. Had this impacted Elaine more than she or I had ever known? Did this result in some deep trauma? Did she now find it hard to form relationships with people, or trust others, or even recognize friend from foe?

On a night out with colleagues, Elaine once mentioned an incident that happened when she had just turned eighteen. She'd worked hard in a nursery that summer and saved a thousand pounds. This money was going to help her get through her first year at Robert Gordon University, one of Aberdeen's two universities. She had saved this money in a jar she kept in her bedroom. One day, she went to count the money, but it was gone. She was devastated and knew someone in her family had taken it. Eventually her brother admitted to taking it to pay for a gambling debt.

"What did you do when you discovered the money had gone? Did you press charges or insist on him paying the money back?" we all asked. Elaine didn't want to go into too much detail, but it seemed that family loyalty and the perceived shame of going to the police had stopped her from getting her money back. She told us she vowed never to speak to her brother again, a promise she'd kept ever since.

My reaction to this tale strayed into judgment. Another of the Bodhisattva precepts encourages trainees to refrain from being proud of oneself and devaluing others. Who was I to judge Elaine's relationship with her family? But I found myself doing so.

When we organized work social events in the evenings, she rarely attended and would say that she needed to speak to her mother that evening. When she was able to attend, she looked delighted and really threw herself into socializing with her colleagues. She could be such good fun. It was hard not to notice, though, that on these occasions her mother would phone her several times during the evening and ask how she was and what was happening. No harm in this, but it always struck me as unhealthy and needy.

I wondered if I could have done something earlier to prevent her reaching this point, but I dismissed the idea quickly. I'd always been fair to Elaine and talked to her with respect. I could understand her disappointment at missing out on a promotion she thought was due to her; however, she should have reflected on the reasons I didn't promote her and learned from this experience. It was her choice to act in this way, and as I pondered her actions, I saw clearly that she was responsible for them, not me.

To be honest, difficult staffing situations bothered me on two levels. Firstly, from a Buddhist perspective, I'd committed myself to Buddhist practice and diligently tried to follow the Soto Zen teachings and practice. But I was now taking a course of action that might lead to someone losing their livelihood. Elaine's plan to marry soon and start a family was likely heavily reliant upon her salary. Would a true Buddhist find a more compassionate way to resolve this situation?

Secondly, what did this say about me as a CEO? I know all about imposter syndrome, where an individual doubts their accomplishments and has a persistent internalized fear of being exposed as a fraud despite there being lots of evidence to show the person is in fact successful. I knew that I didn't suffer truly from this syndrome, but I did feel this at times—the fear of being "found out." I'd been the CEO for four years, and there had been great successes along the way, but this was the third major staffing issue I'd faced in the last six months. *Is it me? Is it something I'm doing? What on earth will my chairman and board of directors think?*

These moments of doubt left me feeling strange and uneasy. There's a saying that being a CEO is the loneliest job in the world; well, right at this moment, I could understand that sentiment. Drained, confused, and deflated, I turned off my computer, closed my office door, and headed home. It had been a long day.

Our HR manager conducted her investigation. Morag looked at the evidence and interviewed Elaine, giving her the opportunity to explain why she'd saved files she shouldn't have and why she'd recorded her colleagues without permission. Elaine admitted to creating the DEFCOM1 folder but said she'd saved only two documents into it, the occupational health report and the company policies. She then argued that the other documents had been planted on her computer and that I, along with other leaders in the organization, were out to get her and people like her. By "people like her" she meant people who are lesbian.

When I heard this, I was amazed. Did Elaine seriously think anyone was going to believe this? The fact that she thought the leadership team and I were out to get her made this trickier.

Morag unsurprisingly recommended that a disciplinary hearing be held. Our disciplinary policy states that no member of staff with any involvement in the allegations should make judgment at a disciplinary hearing. As Elaine had alleged the whole leadership team were conspiring against her, our HR manager recommended that the hearing and any subsequent appeal hearing be heard by a board member.

A disciplinary hearing was convened, and our chairman, Norman, agreed to chair the proceedings. Jim and I were the only ones called to give evidence. Elaine's main argument was that I had discriminated against her on the grounds of her sexuality. She claimed I'd told her that the reason she wasn't appointed to the general manager role was because she was thinking about a same-sex marriage and starting a family, and that this was a serious undertaking that meant her head wasn't in the right space to become a senior manager. As well as this, Elaine claimed that everything on her laptop, with two exceptions, had been planted on her computer because of a conspiracy against her, orchestrated by me and my leadership colleagues.

She had downloaded the occupational health report of her colleague because she knew the individual was homosexual and wanted to know why they'd left the company last year. She suspected that I was homophobic and was trying to prove this.

I had been involved in disciplinary situations before in my management career—but never quite like this. It felt surreal that her main arguments against me were that I was discriminatory and plotting against her and seriously brought my character into question. I was certain that her arguments would fall to pieces under questioning, but you can never be certain. For all Elaine's faults, she was not stupid. She was a real expert with IT, and I worried that she'd manipulated files to incriminate me in some way.

That evening, before the disciplinary hearing, I meditated in my Zendo with Beth. We were joined by our trusty dog Fudge, a chocolate-brown working cocker spaniel who often joined me for meditation. I used the flickering flame of the candle on the altar to light a stick of incense. I offered this incense in the formal way, bowing to the Buddha as Beth stood with her hands in gassho at the back of the room. I walked towards the altar and bowed on one knee and offered the incense up to the altar, saying the three homages as I did so: "Homage to the Buddha, Homage to the Dharma, Homage to the Sangha." I stood, bowed, and then made my way back to where I had started, hands held in gassho. "I offer the merits of this incense offering to all beings so that they may find peace. I offer the merits of this incense offering so that my colleague Elaine may find peace."

Beth and I both bowed and took up our meditation seats and meditated for thirty minutes. Fudge wandered around a bit before settling down next to me, nuzzling his wet nose into my hands. I enjoyed his presence and his warmth.

My mind was not at rest that evening. If you sit in meditation long enough and continue to practice over many years, you can really learn about yourself. The key is not to be judgmental or annoyed with thoughts. Minds think; it's just what they do. But if we casually observe the mind and don't attach too much meaning to all it says, we can be liberated and live more freely and at ease. I was aware that evening that my mind was defensive: *I am compassionate, caring, and have only ever tried to do what's right by her.* Now she was saying I had set her up and discriminated against her. *How dare she! How could Elaine perceive me this way? How could she read my intentions so wrongly?* It was hard for me to fathom.

I let these thoughts come and go. This was my ego at play. Reality lies beneath these thoughts, where you find wisdom and compassion. My mind, and to a certain extent my body, was holding a lot of tension and stress, torn between acting defensively and compassionately towards Elaine.

Sometimes practicing compassion is not easy, hence why I offered the merits of my incense offering to Elaine. Offering the merits of your day's practice to a person you are challenged by can help engender a spirit of compassion. The disciplinary hearing was going to be unpleasant, and Elaine was probably frightened about the repercussions if she was dismissed. *Even in these situations*, I thought, *it's possible for Buddhist values to play their part.*

From the perspective of a CEO, the situation deflated me. I came into this role to change the company for the better. I had improved many things but had not appreciated just how many staffing issues there would be, and it made the job far less enjoyable. People can be very challenging, nasty, and unfair. Our company tried to treat people well and always do the right thing, but still some people were never satisfied. The work we do makes a huge social impact, and I struggled with staff who didn't see the huge value in making a real difference in the lives of vulnerable people.

But the Buddha taught that all things are impermanent. These staffing issues were impermanent too and would pass one day. I resolved to hang in there and learn from these situations as best I could.

After the disciplinary hearing took place, Norman dismissed Elaine from her post. He reached his conclusion based on two key points: Elaine admitted to downloading an occupational health report relating to another member of staff, and the act of downloading this document alone was enough to justify her dismissal. Norman found it hard to believe that Elaine had created the DEFCOM1 folder and saved the occupational health report but then hadn't noticed other files being added to the folder over time. He also knew me and the members of the leadership team and had observed our professional conduct over a number of years, and our evident willingness to treat staff fairly made it highly improbable that there was any conspiracy against her.

Norman concluded as well that he didn't believe discrimination had taken place. He stated that as CEO I had implemented several policies that promoted equality and tolerance and noted I'd introduced the wearing of rainbow-colored lanyards to show our support for the LGBTQ community. During regular one-to-one meetings with me, he had learned that I hadn't promoted Elaine on an interim basis because of her refusal to take on work in the past. It had nothing to do with Elaine's sexual orientation.

I hoped Elaine's dismissal would be the end of the matter. How wrong I was.

She appealed the decision, and a hearing was convened the following week. Two other board members agreed to hear the appeal this time. Dan Carnegie, a senior manager with a major bank, had been on the board for three years, and Lorraine Smith, a director of education with a local authority in London prior to retiring to Scotland, had served for five years. On the day of the appeal, Elaine submitted a grievance that was rambling and very unclear. The board told Elaine that they would not hear the grievance owing to the requirement that issues be raised prior to dismissal from the company.

I later saw a copy of her grievance, and it was an incredible read. She stated that I'd been involved in fraud and had manipulated data about the company, representing it in a way that was far better than reality. Thankfully the board saw this for what it was: nonsense. But I felt vulnerable as CEO. People could say anything about me, and if there hadn't been so many experienced professionals on the board, who knows what this type of accusation might have resulted in? In total Elaine raised thirty-two issues in her letter. Each of the thirty-two points had a dedicated paragraph describing in detail the nature of her grievances. Norman asked me to write a response to each one. At the time, this troubled me slightly; I wondered if they were being taken seriously. In hindsight, I realize Norman knew to cover these issues in case anyone accused him in the future of not asking questions about the accusations.

Over the following days and weeks, I thought about the points Elaine had raised. They would surface in my mind as I sat meditating in my Zendo. I never advertised I was a Buddhist at work, although I didn't deliberately hide it; when I took a week's holiday to go on retreat to the monastery, I told people where I was going. No one asked many questions about it, but I wondered what Elaine would think if she saw me now, sitting with Fudge in my Zendo, offering her the merits of my day's practice. Would it change her perception of me? Would it allow her to see that I was never out to do her harm? Would that even matter to her?

The appeal hearing met the week after the disciplinary hearing. I wasn't called as a witness, but I later read the meeting notes. The panel upheld Norman's decision to dismiss Elaine from her post. For whatever reason, she had clearly done something very wrong, and her cover story unraveled quickly under scrutiny. Surely *this* would be the end of the matter.

Unfortunately, that was not the case. We received a letter from Elaine's solicitor, Mr. Sinclair, stating Elaine intended to take us to an employment tribunal. As I stood reading the letter, I was stunned. Surely Elaine could see her arguments were fundamentally flawed. Could she not accept that she had acted inappropriately and accept her dismissal? Clearly not. And how could the legal system be taking the case seriously? Surely everyone could see this was a farce.

This marked the start of what felt like a never-ending process that saw me liaising with our company solicitor, Arthur Wood, every week for nine months. Norman and I met with Arthur shortly after we received the letter from Mr. Sinclair. We went over everything with a fine-tooth comb again, and Arthur asked us to provide several documents, ranging from the notes of the disciplinary and appeal hearings to screenshots of Elaine's DEFCOM1 folder. The letter from Elaine's solicitor made clear that they were claiming Elaine had been discriminated against on the grounds of her sexuality and that she was unfairly dismissed.

We received an offer to attend judicial mediation. In Scotland this provides the opportunity to settle the case before going to a full legal hearing. Basically, Elaine was hoping that we would make a payment to settle out of court, and she would then go away. I would have thought that the answer to this question was an obvious no. Elaine had acted completely inappropriately, so why should we pay money for her wrongdoing?

Arthur outlined the pros and cons of doing this. I learned that such a situation is not straightforward, and I can understand why some companies simply pay dismissed staff so that the problem disappears. Arthur explained that if Elaine accepted a payment of somewhere between £6,000 and £9,000, this would be cheaper than RCC paying the legal costs of a full employment tribunal. Something about Arthur's explanation seemed morally wrong to me. Norman asked for my view on this. I told Norman that I felt Elaine's actions were wrong and that an organization like RCC making a payment to her felt immoral. Norman agreed; he reasoned that we were an ethical organization trying to do social good, and it was important to take a stand against this type of behavior. We rejected the offer of judicial mediation and headed for full tribunal.

The tribunal wanted to know in great detail what our arguments were against specific points. One thing that pleased us was that the sheriff took a dim view of Elaine's claim of discrimination. The sheriff kept asking Elaine's solicitor to provide more evidence of this and eventually set a deadline for the evidence to be produced. Mr. Sinclair dragged his feet to the point of appearing disinterested in the case. Eventually the sheriff ruled out the discrimination aspect. The tribunal was only going to allow Elaine to claim unfair dismissal.

Arthur had acted as the solicitor for RCC for many years now. He never gave his emotions away; he was friendly and approachable but always very professional. Despite this, I got the impression that he too was surprised by Mr. Sinclair's lack of preparedness. I hoped this was a sign that the tribunal would go our way.

I awoke a bit earlier than I would normally on the morning of the tribunal. I washed and donned comfortable clothes for meditating. But first I took Fudge out for his morning walk. We walked for twenty minutes round the fields and moorland on the edge of our village. The wind was blowing, and it was gray and overcast. Being with my carefree Fudge as he bounded about the fields, chasing rabbits, helped me feel grounded.

Once home, I made my way into the Zendo, let Fudge follow me in, and closed the door behind me. I turned and bowed to the Buddha on my altar and picked a stick of incense off the shelf. Lighting the incense, I made an offering at the altar. "Homage to the Buddha, Homage to the Dharma, Homage to the Sangha. May the smoke from this incense permeate all corners of this room and my house and permeate the corners of the world—like the Buddha's teaching permeating all corners of my life and all corners of the world." I bowed to my meditation stool and sat in meditation for thirty minutes. Fudge, tired from his walk, fell asleep at my side, his head resting against my leg.

My mind was busy. My ego could not dismiss the injustice of it all. I let these thoughts come and go. This is the practice of the Soto Zen tradition.

This great practice is extremely liberating. It allows space for tension to ebb and flow. There is no pretense of being a great Buddha, free from all mental anguish. Instead there is an acceptance of humanity, our grasping mind, our ignorance, but also our kindness and compassion. Although my mind was busy and I felt tension everywhere in my body, my meditation that morning allowed me to feel a bit peaceful. I could not control the outcome of the day, but I could choose how I approached it and responded to it.

I determined that I would be honest and never derogatory towards Elaine. I would answer the questions from the sheriff without embellishment and accept the outcome. Beth joined me at the breakfast table, and her chatting eased my tension further. She knew it was a big day for me, and she wished me luck and kissed me goodbye as I left for the tribunal. Fudge walked to the door with me and offered a paw, which I shook as I left, giving him a kiss on the head as well. As I drove to the court in Aberdeen, I tried to be mindful.

Buddhism teaches that to really live well, we must live in this moment. This is where our life really is. This may sound obvious, but how often do we find ourselves reliving the past or imagining the future? It is rare to be fully present in this moment. If we can be present in our life, it takes on a lighter, more peaceful quality. As I drove, I noticed the dark, brooding sky and the trees being blown in the wind. Even though I was headed towards an unpleasant day, I saw the world's beauty and felt grateful to be part of its drama.

I parked and made my way to the court. On arriving, I had to pass through a security check and was shown to a room where Arthur awaited me. He talked me through how the day would proceed. I was going to be called first. I'd be questioned by Elaine's solicitor and then by Arthur. The sheriff might ask supplementary questions. After I had given evidence, I'd be allowed to sit next to Arthur to give instruction in my capacity as CEO.

After a few minutes, the court clerk arrived and called for Arthur to come through. I was called five minutes later. Entering the court, I was asked to sit in a chair behind a desk. On my right sat the sheriff, who was flanked by two laypeople. In Scotland, employment tribunals always have two laypeople to support the sheriff. One layperson has a human resources background, and the other is usually a trade union representative of some kind. The idea is that they bring balance to the proceedings, providing an employer and employee perspective. This aids the sheriff when making a final decision on the case.

To my left were two more desks. At the first sat Elaine with her solicitor, Mr. Sinclair. At the next desk sat Arthur with an empty chair next to him, which I would take once I had finished giving evidence. Now that I was in the chair, I felt relaxed.

Mr. Sinclair began asking questions about the events that led up to Elaine's dismissal. The questions initially seemed routine, and I answered them honestly, as best I could. He then asked questions about a meeting I'd had with Elaine a few weeks before her suspension. I started to answer, but Mr. Sinclair jumped in, "Was it not the case that you stated at that meeting that Elaine had not been promoted because you felt that her coming out as gay and her wishing to start a family meant she was not in the right frame of mind to take on more responsibility?"

Arthur immediately rose to his feet. "Don't answer that. Objection, m'lady. It was agreed that this court would not consider any claim of discrimination. I therefore ask that my client is not asked any questions in relation to discrimination."

Mr. Sinclair laughed and said, "Surely these points are relevant to the case and the court must hear Mr. McKenzie's answers on what was said at this meeting." There was a long pause as the sheriff considered how to proceed. This was important, and although I knew that I had never acted inappropriately towards Elaine, I had a feeling this might be a long day if the sheriff allowed questions on discrimination.

The sheriff spoke. "Mr. Sinclair, it has been decided that this case is only about unfair dismissal and not discrimination. We have discussed at length that there is no evidence to support that claim, hence why it is not part of the case being heard today. I ask that you do not question Mr. McKenzie further in this regard."

Both Elaine and Mr. Sinclair looked shell shocked. My suspicions that Elaine and her solicitor had never really grasped the complexities of this case looked well founded. It was clear from Elaine's demeanor that she knew this was a difficult arena to be in. This was a small early victory, but I was not out of the woods yet. I proceeded to answer questions, and I felt that all my answers showed the absurdity of Elaine's position. Throughout, I was careful never to attack Elaine personally and referred to her with dignity whilst still pointing out what I felt were inappropriate behaviors and actions she had displayed.

Before I knew it, my time on the stand was over. I was surprised when I looked at my watch and saw that two hours had passed. I believed I had answered the questions well, and Elaine's solicitor seemed to be on the back foot. Elaine looked awkward, like a small girl sitting in a room full of adults. She fidgeted nervously in her seat and regularly turned to whisper in her solicitor's ear.

Next up was Norman. Our chairman received questions about his handling of the disciplinary hearing and his decision to dismiss Elaine from her post. A very experienced professional, he had been in these situations before so knew how to handle himself. He was also a very moral character who had no interest in hurting Elaine. His answers were precise and fair. Never did he make any remarks aimed at Elaine's character; he kept everything factual and cordial. Norman was on the stand for an hour and a half. At the end of his evidence, the sheriff called for another thirty-minute break.

During the break, I bumped into Elaine in the corridor. We both mustered a nod and a smile. There was no point in being bitter even in this strangest of situations.

As we resumed, next up on the stand was Morag, our HR manager. Her evidence didn't last long, approximately thirty minutes or so. Before we knew it, the day was over. Before leaving, the sheriff laid out what would happen the next day. Proceedings would reconvene at 10 a.m., and Elaine would take the stand. I asked Arthur how he felt that first day had gone. He replied, "I would say that was a bad day for Elaine."

I was the first of the family to arrive home. Fudge greeted me at the door with his usual offer of a paw, which I shook before giving him a hug. My trusty dog was always glad to see me, and his greeting filled me with joy. We made our way up to the Zendo, and I burned incense, offering the merits of my meditation to Elaine. "Homage to the Buddha, Homage to the Dharma, Homage to the Sangha. I offer the merits of this incense offering to Elaine and hope that the merits of my meditation can help her be at peace." I took my place on the bench and meditated for thirty minutes.

I expected my mind to be a busy place after the stresses of the day. I was aware of being grateful that the day had gone well for the RCC side. There were angry thoughts in there—some thoughts about winning and being right and Elaine being wrong. Feelings of hurt and annoyance at Elaine for putting me and others through this. But also feelings of compassion towards Elaine. Was she deluded? Was she mentally unwell? How much was this costing her and her partner? How did this young woman get herself into this position?

The chaos did settle from time to time, and for moments I sat and experienced that deeper peace that hovers below the show of the mind.

The next day arrived, and after walking Fudge, morning meditation, and some breakfast, I was ready to attend the hearing and listen to Elaine's evidence. I prepared myself for a day of listening to all sorts of stories about me. With me not being able to answer back or challenge Elaine, this was likely to be a difficult experience. Arthur could challenge, of course, but him doing this on my behalf would feel strange.

When I arrived at the court, Arthur was nowhere to be seen. It was only 9:45, and the court wasn't due to sit until 10, so I presumed he was running a bit late. I sat until 10:10 a.m., which I thought was a bit odd. Then the court clerk came in to see me and informed me that the sheriff had delayed the start of the hearing as Elaine's solicitor had asked to speak to Arthur about the best way forward. They were now in talks. I had no idea what this meant.

Eventually Arthur entered the room. "There's been a development. Elaine doesn't want to take the stand and has offered to drop the case as long as RCC pay her legal costs."

"She doesn't want to take the stand?" At this point, anger rose within me. Elaine had put us all through months of hassle, worry, and legal costs because she felt so aggrieved at how she had been treated by me and the company, and now that we had gotten to this moment, she didn't want to take the stand. I was dumbfounded. *What does this mean?*

Arthur explained that basically Mr. Sinclair and Elaine felt yesterday had gone so badly for them that there was no point in her taking the stand. My impression of Elaine as a small girl in a room full of adults had been correct. She had heard the evidence in the clinical, stark environment of the court and realized her arguments were unfounded. She had been deluded all along, and the courtroom provided the clarity she needed in order to see this for herself. Elaine knew that if she took the stand today, she was going to look like a fool making petty arguments that lacked any rationale.

I thought of the cost to RCC. We are a charity; we don't have a lot of money. The legal bill was already over £10,000 just to prepare for the tribunal and Arthur's first day at the hearing. This was a lot of money, especially when there was absolutely no justification for Elaine's actions. But now she was asking us to pay her legal expenses as well, despite her being the one that had brought this situation upon us all. I had to take a deep breath at this point. My mind conjured up stories of how bad Elaine was, and I reminded myself of the commitment I'd made in my Zendo that morning to approach this as compassionately as I could. I took a deep breath and gently tried to stop my mind from racing away with unhelpful negative thoughts.

"Okay, Arthur, I get why she wants to pull out. We could all see how yesterday went for Elaine. But I really don't see why we should pay her legal fees and expenses. What would these costs be for, exactly, and what is your view?"

"It would be to pay for Elaine's travel here from Wales and her accommodation costs as well as the legal fees incurred throughout the whole process of getting to the hearing. I have not calculated the exact cost as I'd have to ask for some details from Mr. Sinclair. Before I did that, I wanted to check that this was something you were willing to consider. As a rough estimate, I would guess these costs would be something between £5,000 and £8,000."

I had to stop myself from laughing out loud, but I was angry. How could Elaine look herself in the mirror, knowing that she was in the wrong in this situation and costing our organization thousands of pounds?

I told Arthur that I wanted to chat this through with Norman. I called Norman and explained the situation and that my gut feeling was that we should not pay Elaine's expenses; our position should instead be that if Elaine dropped her claim entirely, we would not pursue her for damages. In Scotland, the amount of damages you can claim in this situation is minimal, but I guessed that Elaine didn't want us chasing her for this. Norman agreed. He also felt strongly that Elaine asking us to pay anything was cheek, considering this was all her own doing. I instructed Arthur on how we wanted to proceed and waited to hear what Elaine and her solicitor had to say.

The answer came back quicker than I expected. Elaine had accepted our position. Arthur got the impression that she was desperate not to incur further costs.

Elaine had done inexcusable things, and only she will ever know what possessed her to act in this way, but however much I despaired and stewed over her actions, I recognized that she was human, and part of the human condition is that we make mistakes. Okay, this was a big mistake, but a mistake it was. She had already paid dearly for her actions. She had lost her job and moved back to Wales with her partner because of this. I heard that she had picked up work in an office in a junior role; her income must have dropped significantly. I had no issue with her partner, and I didn't want to be responsible for inflicting more punishment by pursuing Elaine through the courts for damages. She had caused enough pain.

At the start of the tribunal, Mr. Sinclair had raised an issue with the sheriff about the level of compensation Elaine was expecting. The sum was about £70,000, which was broken down into quantities due for various reasons. The most notable line item was £30,000 for injury to Elaine's feelings. How incredible! Nobody at RCC had impugned Elaine's character; we had just presented the facts that proved her wrongdoing. On the other hand, Elaine had accused me of discriminating against her, unfair dismissal, and made all sorts of outlandish accusations about me defrauding the organization. Yet somehow she was demanding £30,000 for injury to *her* feelings!

Mr. Sinclair had pointed out to the sheriff that they still had not factored in the money lost in pension payments. They wanted to calculate this and add it to the total sum. I was on the stand at this point, looking directly at Elaine, and saw a smug look on her face. I have no doubt that she was thinking about the large sum she expected to collect.

Now I thought about Elaine phoning her partner, explaining that she had withdrawn her case before taking the stand. Not only that, but she had received no compensation from the tribunal and was coming home with a large legal bill of her own. That must have been a difficult phone call.

It was hard not to feel a sense of satisfaction that day. I'd experienced the buildup to the tribunal as stressful and unfair, but as I had hoped, the truth had been revealed in the end, and common sense prevailed. I thought about the Bodhisattva precepts, and two of them stuck out for me: "Refrain from speaking about others" and "Refrain from being proud of yourself and devaluing others." Had I lived by these during this ordeal with Elaine? Not entirely, to be honest, although I had tried. My sense of winning the day felt slightly wrong and was not the most appropriate response, but it was there all the same.

Still, I had never badmouthed Elaine and had always tried to speak about her as fairly as I could. Back at RCC, staff never heard me discuss her negatively after her dismissal or after the tribunal. In front of others, I always genuinely recognized the contribution Elaine had made to our organization over the years. I felt okay with my conduct overall. Compassion is the key. Never get frustrated in meditation or life when you get caught up in thoughts. Just gently come back to the moment. My life of practice has been aimed at trying to bring this meditative mind into all that I do, even employment tribunals.

Many thoughts had come and gone throughout this difficult episode. Some thoughts were skillful and some unskillful. But I tried to stay present as best as I could and act from my Buddha nature, my deeper self, my true self, which is found deeper than the thin veneer of my worldly identity as Hamish the CEO.

That evening, I meditated in my Zendo. My mind was full of relief that the tribunal had finished. These thoughts dispersed quickly, my mind stilled, and I felt a peace that seemed to touch the deepest corners of my being. For a short while, I achieved a clarity I have rarely experienced prior to or since that moment. The whole world went quiet, and I felt connected to all beings. I saw how miniscule and unimportant I was. I was one human struggling through life, just like the other eight billion of my fellow humans who share this planet with me. I was aware of all the non-human beings in the world, from birds to insects, all trying to make their way. I was aware of Earth floating somewhere on an outer rim of a spiral tentacle of the Milky Way galaxy. I was aware of the Milky Way as a small cluster of stars in a never-ending universe full of spiral galaxies that look like mist illuminated against a dark sky, going on forever, beyond comprehension.

My inadequacies dropped away, and it seemed like everything was as it should be. I was a Buddhist CEO trying to practice "the way" as best I could. Elaine was a fellow human. We both carried our own baggage, but we were connected as all beings are connected. For a moment I shared that connectedness with Elaine and all others. I saw again how small I am. This was not a scary realization in the slightest. Instead it made me feel that I was part of a bigger whole, and all I had to do was take the next step and keep trying my best, however feeble those steps might be. It was enough to be present and accept my mistakes along the way.

The bell rang: *ting, ting*. Fudge lifted his head from my knee and licked my hands a few times. I stood and bowed to my mat, turned, and bowed to the world. Tears in my eyes and a deep sense of gratitude pumping through my veins, I sank to my knees, looking at the Buddha, the dancing candle flame illuminating his face. I cried and cried for several minutes, tears of joy. Fudge nestled his head against my leg, recognizing my tears.

A Buddhist story came to my mind that evening. Two monks were walking back to their monastery in ancient China and had to cross a river by foot. The water was quite high after recent rain. A woman was nearby, and she was scared to cross. One of the monks kindly carried the woman to the other side. The woman was grateful for his kindness. As they walked on, the monk who carried the woman across the river realized his companion looked troubled.

"What is wrong?" he asked.

"As monks, we are not supposed to have contact with women, but you picked up that woman and carried her."

The monk replied, "I put that woman down when I reached the riverbank, but you are still carrying her."

It was time for me to put Elaine down and get on with my life. Tomorrow would be a new day, and this chapter of my CEO journey was over. Others would surely begin.

CHAPTER 3

My Buddhist Journey

THE BODHISATTVA VOWS

Beings are numberless. I vow to save them.

Desires are inexhaustible,
I vow to transform them.

The Dharma is limitless,
I vow to understand it.

The Buddha's truth is infinite,
I vow to attain it.

Buddhism interested me from a young age. I can't pinpoint when this interest first developed. I remember being intrigued by religious imagery, but something about the Buddha struck me more than any other religious figure. I would ask myself, *Who is the Buddha? Why does he look so peaceful? Is he a god?* This passing interest stayed with me as I moved into my late teens and early twenties. I read introductory books, the usual staples of Alan Watts and D. T. Suzuki, and I eventually went on to attend some classes at university on how to meditate.

By my early twenties, I had a reasonable grasp of what Buddhism was about and tried to meditate a few times a week. At this point I certainly didn't consider myself to be a Buddhist, merely someone with a passing interest. But I did realize the power of meditation. There was no doubt that I felt different on the days I meditated. I felt more compassionate, grounded, and grateful for the world around me. This wasn't a huge moment of realization for me—more a subtle change in my awareness that I enjoyed and appreciated.

I met Beth when I was twenty, and we fell in love instantly. I was studying social work and management, and she was studying nursing. Beth was out having a drink with friends one night in one of the many bars the students' union boasted, Elrond's Palace, named after the character from *The Lord of the Rings*. Images of Elrond the high elf as well as other themes from the book were painted on the walls, but it was otherwise a standard student bar. I was there with a few of my university friends, and our two groups ended up sitting near each other. As typical young men and women in the days before Tinder when people still spoke to each other, we began chatting after a few drinks.

By a stroke of good fortune, I started speaking to Beth. I wasn't known for being a smooth talker. I'd had a few girlfriends in the past, but never anything serious, and I had not dated much past four or five months. This was about to change.

We clicked from the first moment. I had often wondered how people could fall in love and feel so comfortable with each other almost immediately. Whatever happened that night, we both felt it. We talked about everything and anything. It was a meeting of both minds and chemistry, and we knew it within five minutes.

We jumped right into questions about our lives. What did we enjoy in life? Where were our favorite places to eat? Our favorite places to drink? Did we have brothers and sisters? Where were we born? What were our likes and dislikes? *My God*, I thought, *who is this amazing woman?* If I remember correctly, our friends got fed up with us gazing into each other's eyes, and they all headed off to a nightclub and left us to it.

This was the start of a truly glorious romance. That first evening, we went back to Beth's flat and sat up drinking and telling each other stories until the early hours of the morning. I slept on Beth's sofa, although we both found it difficult to keep our hands off each other. We intuitively knew that intimacy would come and wanted to take our time, get to know one another, and let our relationship grow. Looking back, that night still seems perfect to me.

Beth was the most beautiful woman I'd ever seen. She was about five foot seven, and her long brown hair flowed over her shoulders and almost halfway down her back. She had a very slim body. Her face was thin, with striking, dark-green eyes and a smile that melted my heart. But she also possessed something more important to me than looks.

Beth was kind, caring, spiritual, and like me had a real interest in the world around us. We both loved being outdoors and walking, whether that be along the beach or rugged coastline or up in the mountains. Luckily the northeast of Scotland has an abundance of wild areas to walk in. Beth did yoga, practiced Reiki, and occasionally meditated. She was very encouraging of my interest in Buddhism and my meditation.

Four months after we first met, we rented a flat together on Urquhart Road, not far from the city center of Aberdeen and close to Aberdeen's fantastic beach. In the summer months, we would get up early, sometimes as early as 6 a.m., when the city was quiet and walk hand in hand down to the beach. If it was dry, we would spread out a towel on the sand, or sometimes we'd find a rock or a washed-up tree trunk to perch on. Sometimes we meditated together, or Beth might do yoga by my side as I meditated. Both of us loved these precious moments—deeply in love, living in the moment, absorbing each other's company.

Once our meditations were over, we would walk along the beach, seeking things of interest. Over the years we witnessed great sights: dolphins rising out of the sea in large pods; gannets plunging into the sea from great heights as they hunted for fish; terns diving elegantly; short-eared owls returning home from a night's hunting; crabs and shells of all descriptions; distant boats of fishermen and huge supply ships of oilmen. The wind in our faces, we took it all in, perfect as it was.

Sometimes, when we could afford it, we liked to finish our walk at one of the many beachfront cafés—the Sand Dollar, the Washington, the Promenade, or the Inversnecky. We would get a table by the window overlooking the sea and order a vegetarian breakfast to share, washing it down with coffee or a fruit smoothie. Money was tight in our student days, but life was fantastic. We both felt glad to be alive and together.

I contemplate these early days now from my late forties and wonder, *Was I happier then or now?* An interesting thought, and one I find difficult to answer. I have more money and, in the eyes of some, more status now. But though we had little money or status back then, each day was a constant happiness. I suppose, like many of us, we took on different roles as we aged.

Things changed just two years after we met. Beth had not been feeling herself for a couple of weeks, and she didn't know what it was. When we went walking, she lost her breath quickly and complained of a tight feeling in her abdomen. Then she missed her period, which was usually very regular. A pregnancy test confirmed what we eventually suspected; Beth wasn't sick. She was pregnant.

We were shocked. We walked around in a daze for a couple of days, unable to believe it. The strongest emotion was happiness, but it was confusing. We loved each other deeply, and we knew kids were probably going to happen one day. But we were young, just twenty-two, carefree, both in our final year of university. We lived in a rented one-bedroom flat and had little money. When the reality of the situation dawned on us, we felt a little scared about the future.

We worried about what it would do to us as a young, happy couple. The situation brought home to us that we were young hippies, really, without a care in the world, and we were loving life and each other's love, friendship, and company. We were determined not to let this change. After a week, we felt more settled about the situation and regained our composure. This baby had been created in love, and he or she would be born into love. We didn't know anything about being parents, but millions of our fellow humans had done it successfully before us, so why couldn't we? The baby was just the next chapter of our story, and we were going to embrace it as best we could. We resolved to tell our families that week, and maybe that was scarier than anything else.

Beth would finish her nursing degree right before the baby was born, and I would complete my degree just a few weeks later. Though things might be financially tight, we were determined to stay positive. However, just as we began to fully accept the fact that we were going to be parents, another surprise presented itself. I accompanied Beth to her first scan and still remember how excited we were. The sonographer invited us into the small, dark room.

"Hi, I'm Chloe," she said. "Come on in and hop up on the couch." Beth lay on the couch with her pregnant abdomen exposed as Chloe began the ultrasound scan. The cold gel on Beth's skin made her jump, and then we focused intently on the screen before us. It was blurry, and we couldn't really work out what we were seeing.

"Oh, that's interesting," said Chloe, "very interesting indeed." This seemed an odd phrase to use. *Surely Chloe sees babies every day, so why would this scan be particularly interesting?* My heart sank.

"This might come as a bit of a surprise to you both, but you are not expecting just one baby. You're expecting two!"

Beth and I looked at each other in shock. Two babies?

It took some time to sink in, but we felt excited, scared, and delighted all at the same time. We were blissfully ignorant of what lay ahead.

Life changed gradually throughout Beth's pregnancy. We still went for walks together, holding hands as we took in the world around us. Our love only grew during this time. I admired how Beth coped with pregnancy. Never once did she complain, but as time progressed, I could tell that she tired more quickly than normal, she struggled to sleep, and some mornings she suffered from morning sickness. Although our children had not yet arrived, they were making themselves heard.

Time passed, and our baby boys, Angus and Bruce McKenzie, were born on 26 April 1994. Angus was a very healthy six pounds, and Bruce was five pounds, eight ounces, and thankfully both boys and Beth were healthy after the birth with no major side effects to worry about. Like most parents, we were thrilled with their arrival but also a little perplexed. A new world of routines, baths, nappies, breastfeeding, and broken sleep opened up to us. We were happy but very tired, and the realization that our lives had changed forever finally hit us. The early-morning walks and meditations on the beach stopped, as did the carefree lifestyle we once enjoyed together.

Beth, my soul mate, could detect I was a bit down in the first few months after the boys' births. Don't get me wrong; I loved my sons and was still reasonably happy, but I wasn't on my A game.

I had landed my first proper job shortly after graduating and was working with a local social work department, arranging after-care packages for people who'd been discharged from hospital after receiving cancer treatment. I made sure families had all they needed, from transport home to social and medical support in the community. Beth had finished her nursing degree and, once the boys were six months old, found a job working two night shifts a week at Aberdeen Royal Infirmary Hospital. It was ideal; I could look after the boys while Beth worked and slept. Our jobs made all the difference to us financially, and we were able to move into a modest three-bedroom house in Stonehaven, a lovely coastal village just fifteen miles south of Aberdeen city. Still, I wasn't meditating as regularly as I once was, and life, although good, had lost a bit of its sparkle.

Beth was reading the local paper, the *Press and Journal*, one morning and noticed an advert: *Soto Zen Buddhism Meditation Group. New members welcome. Meetings every Monday night 6:30 p.m. in the Quaker's Meeting Hall, Crown Street, Aberdeen.* It said that anyone interested in finding out more about Soto Zen Buddhism were welcome to drop in any week. Beth cut it out and set it aside, thinking this might be just what I needed to rekindle my connection with the world.

I arrived back at the flat that night after a good day at work, and Beth had prepared a lovely vegetarian meal for us: vegetable stir fry served with noodles, and some lovely crusty bread served with a refreshing glass of cold lemon water. The boys were in bed, and we enjoyed the meal together. We didn't say much, merely relished the strong bond between us as we ate. Afterwards, I did the washing up and made us both a cup of tea, served with a chocolate biscuit.

As I sat down, Beth said, "I found something today in the paper I thought might be of interest to you—an advert for a Zen group that meets in Aberdeen."

"Really?" I said. "I didn't know there was a Zen group in Aberdeen. Very interesting."

"Well, I think you should go and check it out next Monday. You don't meditate as much as you used to, and you're not quite yourself these days, so I think it would do you good. You've always said that you felt Buddhist books can only take you so far and you really need a teacher to learn Buddhism properly. Maybe they have a teacher. Who knows?" Beth went on, "What's that saying you always read out when you come across it? 'When the student is ready, the teacher appears.'"

I woke up on Monday morning with a sense of excitement. Would the Buddhist group be good? Would I enjoy it and find it useful? I was intrigued to find out more. I made a quick breakfast for us both: toast with honey, an apple each, and some herbal tea. Angus and Bruce were only a few months old and still breastfeeding, and they fed quite happily that morning as Beth and I ate.

"I hope that your visit to the Buddhist group goes well tonight, my love," said Beth.

"I hope so too," I replied. "I'm really not sure what to expect." Beth walked to the door of our flat with me, Angus and Bruce in her arms. I gave them all a big kiss, which made Angus smile and Bruce frown, and then headed out the door to work.

My day passed quickly, and before I knew it, 5 p.m. had arrived, giving me an hour or so to get some food before heading to the Buddhist group. My office was in Seaton, an area close to the

University of Aberdeen, so I went to Kilau Coffee, a popular café with students and academic staff alike. I had frequented it often in my student days. Ordering a small meal, I wondered what the Buddhist group would be like, having no idea of the impact this night would have on my life.

I finished my meal, paid my bill, and walked into Aberdeen city center, up to Union Street, Aberdeen's high street. I came to Crown Street and turned left, looking for the Quaker Meeting Hall. Like much of Aberdeen, the buildings on Crown Street are constructed from granite. Aberdeen is often called the Silver City on account of the sparkle of those gray granite buildings on a sunny day. Of course, most days in Aberdeen are overcast and cloudy, and the whole place can look quite gray and drab; but on those rare sunny days, it really does have a magical quality.

The Quaker Hall sat between residential flats on its left and a commercial motorbike sales company on its right. For some reason, I felt slightly nervous as I walked through the small car park to the door of the hall.

The door was old, wooden, and painted dark blue. It felt ancient. I walked through it into a vestibule area with beautiful, old wooden paneling around the lower half of the walls and a tiled floor. The walls were covered in posters and announcements that clearly belonged to the Quakers. Nobody was in the vestibule, but I heard voices coming from another room. I made my way through another door that took me to a short corridor. There was a door on my right and one straight ahead, but the voices came from the room on the right. Again, I felt slightly nervous, but I followed the voices into a large hall with chairs all around it. I was immediately struck by a sense of peacefulness and had a feeling this room had been well used over the years by the Quakers.

Two figures, both men, turned to face me. One was dressed in brown robes and had a shaved head. *Could this be a monk?* I wondered.

The other man spoke first. "Welcome. My name is Martin,

and this is Reverend Riku." At this point, they both pressed their palms together, bowed their heads slightly, and smiled. Later I was to find out that this gesture in Japanese is called making gassho. I felt slightly awkward and held my hands up, mimicking the gesture they had made to me. Martin then said, "I presume you're here for the Buddhist group?"

"Yes," I replied.

"Splendid," said Martin, "and a very warm welcome to you. You have picked a great night to come along. We have Reverend Riku with us. He is a monk trained at Throssel Hole Buddhist Abbey and is now the prior at Portobello Priory in Edinburgh, which our Aberdeen group is affiliated to. So, in a way, he's the Soto Zen monk for Scotland."

Reverend Riku smiled a cheeky grin at me and asked, "What's your name?"

"Hamish," I replied.

"I'm so glad that you have come along to visit us tonight. I hope you find it useful," said Reverend Riku.

"I'm sure I will. I'm looking forward to finding out more."

Martin explained that they were setting up the ceremony hall for the Buddhist meeting. They had rented this room every Monday evening from the Quakers for over twenty years. The Quakers were supportive of their meeting house being used by Buddhists and other faiths; all they asked was that we leave the room as we found it.

I helped Martin and Reverend Riku move chairs and tables and set up a Buddhist altar. In minutes, the room was transformed and ready. Rows of five chairs lined two sides. Each chair held a slim book and faced the middle of the room. On the third side of the room stood the beautiful altar, and on the fourth side a single chair that I presumed was for the reverend. The table had been covered with a striking gold-and-purple throw, which transformed the simple table into something elegant. A Buddha statue sat slightly higher than the rest of the items on the table. In front of the Buddha was a small, ornate cup almost overflowing with water. On the left, a bunch of flowers sprouted from a jar, and on the right was a candle, which had just been lit.

Martin turned off some of the lights, giving the room an even more peaceful and esoteric quality. He explained that there would be a short ceremony and the reading of a scripture and then two periods of meditation, followed by a talk from Reverend Riku. We would have a chance to ask questions and discuss what had been said. He then explained that after the ceremony, he and I could leave the ceremony hall and make our way to another room where he could tell me more about the group and all the ways to get involved.

I'd been made to feel so welcome by Martin and Riku and was now both relaxed and excited to be part of an actual Buddhist ceremony led by a Buddhist monk. I had read a lot about Buddhism and read teachings by monks, but I had not expected to meet one this evening, in my hometown.

Now that the room had been set up as a Buddhist ceremony hall, Martin explained, we needed to take off our shoes as a sign of respect, as is done in Zen ceremony halls across the globe. Others started to arrive, and I was introduced to a string of people as they came through the door. Every one of them raised their hands in gassho and welcomed me warmly.

As everyone entered the hall, shoeless, they bowed respectfully towards the Buddha statue on the altar. Feeling slightly self-conscious, I bowed as well. We all took a seat and placed the thin book carefully on the floor beside us. There was a stillness in the room, a deep sense of harmony. I wondered how often this room had been used by the Quakers for their silent meetings and for how many years. I sensed a lot of wisdom in this room, as though it had witnessed much deep contemplation in its time.

A bell sounded from outside the door. Holding incense, Reverend Riku walked in followed by someone I'd just met in the vestibule, carrying a bell. *Ting, ting.* They stood in front of a mat laid out a few feet in front of the altar. The scented smoke wafted in my direction.

The bell rang again, and Reverend Riku went to the altar and bent down on one knee. Placing the incense against his head, he spoke the words "Homage to the Buddha, Homage to the Dharma, Homage to the Sangha." He then rose to his feet, his hands held in gassho, and said, "We offer the merits of this incense offering to all beings and hope that they may find their way to the truth." He placed the incense into a small ceramic pot filled with sand, and the stick stood upright.

Riku turned and retraced his steps. A series of bells were rung, and people in the room seemed to know when to bow. The others began to read out, in a serious rhythmic tone, a scripture from the books beside us. The scripture was called "Rules for Meditation." I followed the words as best I could, speaking quietly. I couldn't take my eyes off everyone else in the room. The monk stood still and peaceful in the middle, and the others rarely lifted their eyes from their scripture book. Once the scripture had been recited, more bells were rung, quietly, and there were more bows before the monk turned to everyone and simply said, "Meditation."

As the others prepared for their meditation, Martin led me through to another room. Two chairs faced each other in the center. An ornate window was lit by the sun, casting a beautiful orange light across the room. Although I didn't fully understand what I had just been a part of, the ceremony had left an impression on me. I felt grounded and like I had taken part in something worthwhile.

Martin explained a bit about the group and its history. The group was affiliated with the Order of Buddhist Contemplatives, known as the OBC, formed by the late Reverend Jiyu Kennet. She founded two large training monasteries in the UK and the US. Over the years, the congregation had grown, as had the interest in Buddhism amongst Western people. As this interest grew, the monks recognized that not everyone could travel to the main monasteries for teaching. So groups had sprung up across the UK, Europe, and the US, and the OBC made a commitment to ensure that monks would be assigned to help support these groups and make the Buddhist teaching available to all people.

Martin went on to explain some of the central tenets of Zen Buddhist teaching. The Buddha described human existence as characterized by suffering. This doesn't necessarily mean that people walk around experiencing pain or a deep sense of anguish. Martin explained that the Buddha referred to a general sense of unease, a quality of never quite feeling satisfied or being fully content with life or what we have. Zen Buddhist practice shows us how to live well and how to free ourselves from suffering. Central to Zen practice is the idea that all beings have what is known as a Buddha nature—the natural sense of being that exists in us all. If we can give up our desires and cease clinging to the world, we can live from a place of wisdom and compassion.

Buddha taught that we are made up of the five skandhas: form, sensation, thought, mental activity, and consciousness. If we truly penetrate our existence, we come to realize that there is no fixed self or identity. The way to experience our Buddha nature is through Zen practice. This practice can be learned by anyone and basically is made up of meditation and mindfulness alongside practicing compassion and living a good life where we cause as little harm to others as possible. Martin laughed at this point and asked, "How did you find that explanation? Did it make any sense?"

I explained that I'd read books on Buddhism, and much of what he'd said made a lot of sense to me. I told him that I meditated when I could, but I was intrigued by his use of the terms *practice* and *developing a practice* and said I was keen to find out more about this idea. He smiled and said, "Let me suggest you keep those questions for later this evening when you can ask Reverend Riku. We are lucky to have a monk that visits us regularly, and I'm sure he will do your question more justice than me. You said that you meditate already. Can I ask, how do you meditate?"

I told Martin that I would sit on the edge of my bed or the edge of a sofa, with my hands lying flat on my thighs and my eyes closed, and I would normally count my breath, breathing in, then out slowly, counting *One, two*, etc. Sometimes I said words to myself as I breathed in and out. As I inhaled fully, I might think, *Peace*; then, as I fully exhaled, I might think, *Calm* or *Love*.

Martin commented that this is good practice and that I clearly had a good grounding in meditation. However, he said in Soto Zen we practice a particular form of meditation that is often called "just sitting"; in Japanese it is referred to as *shikantaza*. In this there is no particular focus, such as the breath, counting, or using certain words. We just sit, allowing thoughts to come and go and trying not to get attached to them. Our minds do wander and begin to engage with the world. If we find ourselves thinking about what will happen tomorrow, what we will have for dinner, or any other thought, we compassionately draw our attention back to just sitting, time and time again.

"The practice can seem simple, but in my own life I've found it to be extremely powerful and helpful. Soto Zen also teaches that the main precepts to follow are the ten Bodhisattva precepts: to refrain from killing; refrain from stealing; refrain from coveting and sexual misconduct; refrain from saying that which is untrue; refrain from selling the wine of delusion and indulging intoxicants; refrain from speaking about others; refrain from being mean with either Dharma or wealth; refrain from being proud of yourself and devaluing others; refrain from anger; and refrain from defaming the three Buddhist treasures: the Buddha, the Dharma, the Sangha. 'The Buddha' refers to the historical figure Shakyamuni Gautama, who founded the religion, 'the Dharma' being the Buddha's and other great Buddhists' teachings, and 'the Sangha' being the Buddhist community."

There was little else to be said without overloading me. I was eager to see and experience the meditation in the hall. We quietly made our way back through. The light was dim, and it took a while for my eyes to adjust. The others were all facing the wall. Some sat on cushions with legs folded in the lotus position, some on short benches with their legs tucked under the stool in a kneeling position, giving them an upright posture. Others sat on chairs. There were five people on one side and three on the other, and meditation benches left for me and Martin.

On the far side of the room sat Reverend Riku, who, unlike the others, faced outward as if to observe all those in the room. The Buddha altar looked even more impressive as the candle glowed in the darkness.

I sat on a meditation bench as instructed and felt comfortable and relaxed. Soon I became aware of my thoughts. *What would Beth say if she saw me now? What should I ask Reverend Riku at questions? I wonder if the boys are sleeping.* My instinct was to feel annoyed. I was supposed to be meditating, not thinking like this. But I remembered Martin telling me that compassion is the key, so I gently brought my awareness back to just sitting. I felt grounded and began to relax deeply into the meditation.

The room was silent, very silent. I heard the distant noise of cars, birds singing, and the occasional voice outside on the street. I couldn't put my finger on how I felt, but maybe for the first time ever, I felt connected. Connected to those in the room, connected to something bigger. For a moment, everything was just as it should be.

Before I knew it, a bell rang quietly to signal the end of meditation. People bowed, and another scripture was recited, and then there was some more bowing before the formal part of the meeting was concluded. Martin said to me, "Now it's time for Reverend Riku's talk, tea and biscuits, and questions."

I felt slightly awkward, not knowing quite what to do to help as people moved around. I helped get the chairs into a circle and then sat and waited. Before long, everyone was seated, and someone called Kyle poured tea for everyone, helped by a woman called Mary, who added milk and sugar for those who wanted them. I noticed that Reverend Riku was offered his tea first, and then a plate of biscuits was passed around and Reverend Riku was offered first take. The monk seemed like part of the crowd, but there was clearly respect for him amongst the group. I sipped my tea, totally unaware of how the next twenty minutes would change my life forever.

Reverend Riku smiled at everyone. He was dressed in brown robes, and his head was shaved, so it was difficult to say what color his hair would be. About five foot ten and very slender, he had dark-blue eyes that twinkled, and his face was kind. He laughed often. I got the sense that here was someone at ease with himself and with the world around him.

"Welcome, everyone, good to see you all again, and nice to sit with you all. Also, a warm welcome to Hamish. It's nice to have you with us, and I hope you find it useful.

"Tonight, I'm going to talk about acceptance. Acceptance is an important part of Buddhist practice, and it's something I've thought about recently, particularly in regard to lay practice. As we know, the Buddha explained that humans tend to experience life as suffering. Not necessarily deep suffering, though that is the case for some, but most people feel some level of suffering in their lives. This could be physical or mental. That feeling that if only I didn't have this pain in my leg, my life would be okay. If only I didn't have to work with that colleague, my life would be okay. If only I earned a little more money, then my life would be okay. If only my house were a little bigger, I would be happier. I wish that my holiday were here now and not four months away. If only my kids didn't get up last night. If only I didn't have to change their nappies every day. If only my kids would behave. If only my kids had been born a bit later, I could have saved money and our finances would be better. If only I was not a parent with all this responsibility, I'd be fine. If only my parents weren't sick, I wouldn't have to look after them so much. If only. If only. This is the suffering the Buddha pointed to."

As Reverend Riku spoke, I wondered if he had delved into my mind and glimpsed my inner thoughts. It felt as if his every word spoke to me directly. If only Beth and I had a little bit longer together before the kids came along. How I missed the carefree days and early-morning walks on the beach and being on our own together. Although my life was good in so many ways, in that moment I saw that I didn't often appreciate it, and I certainly recognized how this manifested as suffering.

I listened intently.

"At the heart of Zen teaching is acceptance. Acceptance of our lives as they are. Unfolding each day. I believe there are about eight billion people on this amazing planet we call Earth. Each one of us with our own struggles, our own good times, and our share of bad times. Life cannot play out in the same perfect way for all of us. We are dealt different cards.

"On top of this," he continued, "is the time we live in, the decade and century we are born into, which shapes us in its own way. We have no choice but to live in our time. Our time, for many, is characterized by the pressures of work, the pressure to keep up with the latest in consumer goods, provide the most we can for our families, strive to be promoted or recognized within our profession, to look beautiful, have the perfect body and be fit and healthy and to wear the best clothes in line with the latest fashion. Within all these things there can be happiness. To be fit and healthy and live well is a good thing. To provide for our family is a good thing. To find our work meaningful is a good thing. But for many, this constant pressure and striving to achieve status, over time, wears us down, and we experience life as suffering."

I was spellbound. What he was saying was so simple, but it pointed to my own experience like nothing else I'd ever heard.

The monk continued, "One of the key teachings of Buddhism is to realize that there is a path open to us all that, if followed, can allow us to live free of suffering. Acceptance is key to following this path and way of life. The Buddha taught that we can end suffering through living in this moment and, most importantly, accepting the circumstance of our lives here and now. Through meditation we can cultivate a compassionate outlook on the world and see that whatever our life circumstances may be, we can be free of suffering. The peace that we can all find is not dependent on outside factors, like having perfect health, wealth, or career; it only relies on us accepting our situation, practicing meditation and mindfulness, and trying to apply the Buddhist precepts to our daily life. In Zen we say that everything and everyone has the Buddha nature. For me this is characterized by a sense of peace and contentment wherever we are.

"This way of life does not mean that we become a doormat for others, simply accepting things in our lives that are wrong if we find ourselves in a difficult situation that is unfair. We maybe have a boss who is a bully or are in a relationship that is controlling. I am not saying that we go on blindly accepting this situation. Often in a situation like this, the skillful action to take is to get out of the relationship or find a new job.

"However, acceptance is still the key. Even whilst dealing with difficult situations, we can be accepting: 'This is where I am just now in life. It might be that I need to move on, but I am accepting that here and now, this is what I am dealing with, and I will deal with it from a place of Buddhist practice.' This is an important point. The Zen view is very much that enlightenment is not something esoteric to be found sometime in the future on the top of a mystic mountain. Zen teaches us that enlightenment is to be experienced in every moment, whether good, bad, or indifferent. We just need to practice, live fully in each moment, let our actions come from our Buddha nature, and find an enlightened response to every moment of our life. An enlightened response to the difficult colleague, to the child that wakens you in the middle of the night, to the sick relative or friend that needs your support, and all the other situations that seemingly cause us suffering. If we can find an enlightened response to these situations, then our suffering can end."

Riku continued, "You know that I like a story, so here is one for you tonight, recounting an old Zen tale. Two young novice monks bumped into each other at the river as they were collecting water for their masters. One was the disciple of a Zen Buddhist master and the other of a martial artist. The disciple of the martial artist said that his master could break wood with his bare hands and leap over a house. 'What can your master do?' The Buddhist disciple replied, 'My master eats when he eats and sleeps when he sleeps.'" There was some laughter at this story, and Reverend Riku laughed too. "A simple teaching, but it speaks volumes about the Buddhist approach. Enlightenment, peace, and contentment does not need to be found in fanciful or incredible acts. It is found in everyday life in actions such as eating and sleeping. All we have to do is be fully present to our everyday life."

There was something about that evening that I will never forget—the start of my Buddhist practice, the start of Buddhism becoming a big part of my life. Since that day, I have been a practicing Buddhist and have been part of the Aberdeen Buddhist Sangha for more than twenty-five years. I visit Throssel Hole Buddhist Abbey regularly on retreat and know many of the monks on a first-name basis. I may not be enlightened, but there is no doubt that the Buddhist path has allowed me to experience something I would not have found without it.

I'm still not sure how this Buddhist ended up a CEO, but I have tried my best to live my daily life guided by Buddhism, and this includes my approach to my CEO role, where I've tried to apply compassion in everything I do.

CHAPTER 4

Dreaming of Hermits

I climb the road to Cold Mountain,

The road to Cold Mountain that never ends.

The valleys are long and strewn with stones;

The streams broad and banked with thick grass.

Moss is slippery, though no rain has fallen;

Pines sigh, but it isn't the wind.

Who can break from the snares of the world

And sit with me among the white clouds?

—*Hanshan*

I immediately took to Buddhist practice and felt its benefits in my life. Beth could see these benefits, and although she never became a Buddhist herself, she respected its teaching and was glad it had brought her soul mate some peace and joy.

As time went on, though, the practice caused some issues between us. These issues never became so large that they tarnished our relationship, but for a while I think she was disappointed I'd become so deeply involved; she felt excluded from a part of my life. This was never my intention, but on reflection I can see why she felt that way. We found a way of dealing with this, and as I matured with age and my practice deepened, these issues dropped away. Our love still comes from a deep well, and our roots have intertwined and only grown stronger over the years.

As I began to study Buddhism more deeply, I visited Throssel and got to know monks and other lay trainees. I became more deeply immersed in the practice. It unearthed feelings I hadn't known existed. I became very drawn to the idea of becoming a monk and being a hermit. I can understand why this troubled Beth as these aren't exactly ideal thoughts for a happily married man with two children. But however much I wanted to wish these thoughts away, I couldn't escape them and the deep pull they had on me.

My first six months with the group in Aberdeen saw me attend every Monday night. I embraced the group and everything it offered. I got to know the monk at the Portobello priory in Edinburgh well. Reverend Riku visited the Aberdeen group once every month and ran a retreat that I attended, with meditation and teaching periods. It was great to have the opportunity to form a close relationship with a monk, who just happened to be an ordained Zen master. I was really impressed with the example of his life. What struck me more than anything was just how normal he was. No airs and graces, just a thoughtful, compassionate, and humorous human being.

I learned all about the long and deep history of the Soto Zen tradition and how it had grown out of other traditions, such as Chan Buddhism in China. Ultimately these different Buddhist traditions all flowed back to the historic Buddha, Shakyamuni Gautama, in India way back about 500 BC. After his death, the disciples of Shakyamuni spread his teachings throughout India, and over the centuries these teachings traveled beyond India and into neighboring countries, such as Tibet, China, Thailand, and later into Japan and finally the West, mixing with the existing cultures and religious beliefs of those countries. Buddhist teachings took on a subtly different flavor in each culture, leading to the different Buddhist traditions we see today: Zen, Chan, Therevada, Tibetan, and others. Buddhism also split into two major schools of thought, Hinyana and Mahayana, both with their own view on the best way to practice Buddhism.

For me, the spread of Shakyamuni's teachings shows their true value, which lies in their compassion and wisdom in not being so rigid that they could not be adapted to then add value to the cultures

Buddhism spread to. Although each Buddhist school might have slightly different forms, the fundamental teaching of this great tradition remains the same.

All the sutras and the monks and laypeople that have inspired me along the way talk about their *practice*, which brings me back to the questions that struck me at that first meeting: what is practice, and what does establishing a practice mean? For me, internally, practice has been a way of committing myself to this Buddhist life, a way of making it central to my life, the decisions I make, and how I approach each day and each moment. Buddhist teaching shows us ways to establish a practice and deepen it along the journey.

I get up early every day at 6 a.m. and meditate for thirty minutes. After meditating, I recite several Buddhist scriptures, including the "Scripture of Great Wisdom," followed by reciting the ancestral line of my Soto Zen lineage, and then I say out loud the ten Bodhisattva precepts that remind me of the moral code, explained by the Buddha, by which I aim to live my life. I follow this by offering the merits of my day's practice to someone I know who is suffering in some way. Then I take Fudge out for a contemplative walk before returning home to make myself tea and some breakfast, and if time allows, I read a Buddhist text or poetry.

Doing this each morning helps me establish the right foundation for the day ahead. It helps me to feel grounded, my mind is more relaxed, and I'm not deliberately thinking of all the things I need to do that day. Instead I have started the day just being in the moment of my meditation with my trusty companion Fudge. There are occasions where I don't manage to get up and follow my preferred routine—if I have an early meeting or I'm ill or just haven't slept well. These days are infrequent, but they do happen from time to time. One good thing about not starting the day with meditation is that it shows the value of having a daily practice. On these days I feel different and less grounded and content than the days when I meditate.

I attempt to practice mindfulness and bring Buddhism into all aspects of my day. If time allows, I arrive early at work, then go for a short twenty-minute walk along the banks of the beautiful River Dee. As I walk, I try to be mindful of every step and grateful for what I see and encounter along the way. Fish rise from the depths of the Dee's dark waters, ducks dive for food, dippers bob on rocks, herons stand alert on the riverbanks, and people pass by, heading for work or walking their dogs. I stop occasionally and take a deep breath and am grateful for it all. Back at the office I try to be friendly, kind, and compassionate with my colleagues, and as I walk between offices, I bring my attention to the moment and am aware of each step I take, every movement of my feet and legs as I walk, bringing me fully into each moment of my life.

When I return home at night, I look forward to seeing Beth, the boys, and Fudge. I give Beth a kiss and a hug and am glad to see her beautiful, cheerful face and be her partner in life. I would kiss and hug the boys, but they might not be so grateful. Now that they're in their twenties, they prefer me to say hello. I still occasionally give them a hug to show that I deeply care for them and that as men it's okay for us to show our affection for each other. Fudge always gets a cuddle and kiss, and he never complains!

After reuniting with my family, I shower quickly, change into some loose, comfortable clothes, and enter the Zendo for a short period of meditation. Usually my mind is cluttered with chatter and stories repeating on a loop from the day I've had—who said what, why did he say that, I didn't like that, what should I do about that situation? I might only meditate for about fifteen minutes and finish with reciting Great Master Dogen's "Rules for Meditation." This great scripture, which lays out instructions for how to practice and how to establish a practice within your daily life, was written in the thirteenth century and it is still recited daily by those following the Soto Zen tradition. It amazes me just how relevant Dogen's words are all these years later.

Some of what Dogen writes I find particularly inspiring: "This type of meditation is not something that is done in stages. It is simply the lawful gateway to carefree peace. To train and enlighten ourselves is to become thoroughly wise; the koan appears naturally in daily life. If you become thus utterly free you will be as the water wherein the dragon dwells or as the mountain whereon the tiger roams. Understand clearly that the truth appears naturally and then your mind will be free from doubts and vacillation."

Powerful words to read when my mind and body are still disturbed by the stresses and strains of the day. Fudge almost always joins me in the Zendo and settles down at my side and places his head in my lap. I love his company and miss it when he doesn't join me. He is a great dog, obedient and always by my side.

After meditation, I go downstairs and eat dinner with Beth, the boys joining us if they're around. We normally prepare dinner the night before so it's ready to eat once we come home from work. Before we eat, I make gassho and recite the five thoughts: "We must think deeply of the ways and means by which this food has come. We must consider our merits when accepting it. We must protect ourselves from error by excluding greed from our minds. We will eat lest we become lean and die. We accept this food so that we may become enlightened."

For me this is another simple technique to bring me back to this moment, and it's useful in cultivating a grateful attitude. It's so easy to just hurry down our food and forget to be grateful that we have food. Food and cooking has played a central part of the Soto Zen tradition. The position of head cook, known as *tenzo* in Japanese, is very important in the monastery.

Dogen himself went on a very arduous and dangerous journey across the sea to China, quite an undertaking in the thirteenth century, to visit a Chan Buddhist monastery that would have a profound effect on him. He was struck by the care and attention the monks put into preparing the food for the temple. He was also struck by the fact that the head cook was a senior monk often only outranked in seniority by the abbot of the monastery. He inquired into why this was so and was told that preparing food was an important aspect of Buddhist training and that the cooking of food was an expression of the Buddhist practice as well as an offering to those who eat the food which has been prepared. He was so impressed that he went on to write an important text within the Soto Zen tradition called the *Tenzo Kyokun*, which translates as "Instructions for the Zen Cook."

In his instructions he writes movingly and inspirationally about how to prepare food. Dogen writes, "When you prepare food, never view the ingredients from some commonly held perspective, nor think about them only with your emotions. Maintain an attitude that tries to build great temples from ordinary greens, that expounds the Buddhadharma through the most vital activity." He also writes, "Treat utensils such as tongs and ladles and all other implements and ingredients with equal respect; handle all things with sincerity, picking them up and putting them down with sincerity."

I still read this scripture regularly. At first glance it is perhaps only a list of procedures to be followed whilst preparing food. For me, though, it goes much deeper, and the instructions are really about how to cook your own life. It is very much the Buddhist way to be present to your life, be grateful, and treat the ingredients with respect. Whether it be a soup made with the finest ingredients or one with vegetables that do not look so good, we should use and eat the ingredients with dignity and respect. As in life, there are aspects of our job, family life, friends, and even Buddhist practice that we find more agreeable than others. But if we practice well and cook our life with care, approaching all these aspects of life in a manner that is compassionate, accepting, and grounded, enlightened action is revealed to us in the most mundane of tasks. This is what Dogen is encouraging us to do in his instructions for the Zen cook.

I fell in love with these forms and practices. They took hold of me with such a force of sincerity it surprised me. Although Beth loves me deeply, she and the boys could see that something had changed in me. Many of these changes were positive, but I think we all had to adjust to them. When I clicked with Buddhist practice, my life changed overnight. The world I stepped into every morning when I left the house suddenly felt like a completely different place—a whole new world of gratitude, peace, contentment, joy, and beauty.

Simple daily tasks such as cleaning the house, cooking a meal, shopping, drinking tea, or putting away clothes became acts of joy when done mindfully. I tried to do these daily chores with a contemplative mind, being fully present to each activity. If I was cooking, as I selected the ingredients from the fridge or cupboard I'd be aware of the cold touch of the refrigerator door when I opened it. I'd be aware of the smells coming from the fridge before selecting my ingredients. I'd be aware of the touch, color, and feel of the vegetables and sauces as I picked them up. I'd wash them carefully before preparing them. As I cut or peeled my ingredients, I'd be aware of the knife's blade making the cut, how hard or softly I had to push to make the cut. When stirring the ingredients and adding spices and sauces, I'd be fully aware of the texture of the wooden spoon in my hand, the smells, the stirring action. I'd select spices, herbs, and sauces, careful to add the right amounts to make the meal as tasty and wholesome as possible. I'd be sure to cook the meal as well as I could, not undercooking or overcooking.

I had carried out these daily tasks all my adult life, indifferent to them. I saw them as neither positive nor negative acts, just things that had to be done. Over the years I usually rushed through my chores, thinking about what had happened earlier that day or where I was going that evening. Buddhist practice showed me that these seemingly mundane acts could become expressions of enlightenment. When I found this new way of living, I could hardly believe how grounded and peaceful I felt. The world felt like it had changed forever, and it had.

Meditating brought a different quality to my days. I lived in the moment more; I noticed the little things more. I became more aware of the color of the sky, the birds singing, the small daily kindnesses that are out there, like the old lady holding the door open for me or a car stopping to let me cross the road when it's busy. Over time I became more attuned to other people: their kindness but also their troubles—the heaviness some people carry around with them, the deep sadness in others. I felt more compassionate overall. In no way was I a perfect being, but I felt great and much more compassionate with myself and others.

I also loved the look and feel of my Zendo and all things Buddhist. The smell of the incense, the altar with the Buddha, always sitting there as a reminder of what's possible. My zabuton (meditation mat), which made kneeling to meditate a bit more bearable. My meditation bench, handmade by the monks at Throssel Hole. The atmosphere of the Zendo, which I only used for meditation, became still and quiet, almost as if the intention of my meditation and the peacefulness of the Buddha statue had altered the feel of the room.

I fell in love with the Buddhist life, and I even had my own Buddha dog, always by my side. There are times when it's harder than others. Nights where I haven't slept well and it's a struggle to get up. Days when I'm really stressed with work and my mind never stops chattering during meditation. But I love the discipline of the practice that encourages us to keep sitting in meditation every day despite the challenges of life. Over time you realize that the benefits of this gentle practice are deep and profound.

I recognize there is an irony here. At the heart of Zen Buddhist practice is the teaching of not clinging to ideas or things. The Buddha taught that through clinging to ideas of who we are, or to material things, we lose sight of our true nature. But I was, in a way, clinging to the practice. I'd fallen in love with its forms and now strongly identified as a Buddhist. I try to distance myself from these internal thoughts; Buddhism points to a deeper reality that goes beyond these forms and concepts of being Buddhist. *Buddhism* is just another word, a form, a vehicle to help us realize the truth, but it's not the truth itself. This is an important teaching.

Looking back on my life now, I can appreciate how Beth felt about all the changes my Buddhist practice brought to our lives. Instead of cuddling every morning, she was met by a different routine. I would jump out of bed at 6 a.m., leaving her in bed alone. The sweet smell of incense would slowly permeate the house. She would be aware of me meditating in another room, separate from her. There's no doubt there was a marked change in our routine.

Not only was I absent in the morning, but she noticed other subtle changes. Beth would say I became quieter and less fun than before. Meditating regularly definitely quietened my mind, and I became more comfortable with silence. And as I liked to rise early, I now wanted to go to bed at 10 p.m.

My desire to become a vegetarian also brought some stress. We had two young kids who liked to eat meat, so we tended to make a meal we could all eat. Though Beth and I were not big meat eaters, we did enjoy fish and occasionally ate other meat. A chicken roast on a Sunday and an occasional steak were a treat to look forward to. But the more I practiced Buddhism, the more in tune I felt with other beings, including nonhumans. The idea of eating meat didn't feel right anymore. This made things a bit more complicated. It maybe doesn't sound like much, but when you're tired and have to cook a meal for four and find you're cooking a meat dish for three and a vegetarian meal for one, it can be a bit of a pest.

Likewise, Beth and I weren't big drinkers, but we enjoyed a glass of wine on weekends, and I liked a couple of cold beers on a Saturday night. The desire to drink alcohol also began to diminish the more I meditated regularly. This wasn't planned, and despite a lot of Buddhist teaching encouraging the avoidance of alcohol and meat, being teetotaling and vegetarian isn't mandatory. But it happened naturally through meditating and practicing over time. I felt a clarity and peace I'd never felt before, and drinking seemed to spoil that feeling. Why drink when I felt so good already? Although we still went out with friends, and I enjoyed those evenings, Beth noted that I was subtly different. Quieter, slightly withdrawn, still friendly enough, but less likely to start conversations or crack jokes than I used to be.

Suddenly, her soul mate wasn't there anymore. Her day began by waking on her own. At night she stayed up and watched TV on her own. When she came to bed, I was already asleep. There was no interaction.

On top of these changes were other unexpected twists. My daily practice was in place, but I also began to visit the monastery at Throssel Hole as often as I could. I got to know the monastic community. Until this point in our relationship, we'd always holidayed together as a family, and although this didn't change completely, those family holidays happened less often. We still enjoyed a two-week summer holiday together, occasional time together at Christmas if Beth's shifts allowed, but I built into my routine at least one week's retreat at Throssel Hole each year and at least one long weekend.

Still, Beth never stopped supporting my visits to Throssel, even to this day. My Beth is an amazing woman, and we have never been controlling with each other. Each of us is free to do our own thing. Over the years, Beth has attended her own retreats at the Findhorn Community, shamanic workshops, and Reiki gatherings. I've always encouraged her to enjoy these experiences, and we believe occasionally going our own way deepens our love and life together. However, I can see why she felt that my relationship with Throssel, and my subsequent interest in monks and hermits, was a bit different.

Nothing I have ever done or attended in my life has given me the peace and tranquility that I feel after visiting Throssel Hole. Living with the community of monks for a week is always an incredible experience for me. It wouldn't be to everyone's liking, and the daily schedule to be followed, on the face of it, doesn't seem very relaxing at all. When you arrive, you are greeted warmly by the guest master or one of their assistant monks. You are shown to your room or your place within the meditation hall. Depending on when your retreat officially starts, you normally have an hour or so for quiet time before it begins. I take these moments to soak in the peace. When the retreat begins, a schedule is posted on different notice boards throughout the monastery. The schedule tells you when to get up, where to be when, and what time to go to bed. The rigid routine might seem strict or oppressive to some, but I find it liberating, especially in comparison to my CEO life. For once I don't have to think, plan, instruct, explain, or lead. I just have to be where I'm supposed to be without much thought and do the task I've been given.

Everyone rises at 6 a.m., meditates together, has their meals together, and lights go out at 10 p.m. Everyone is expected to be in bed without exception. In the morning you're woken by a monk ringing a bell. A monk is tasked to walk round the monastery with the bell to ensure everyone is up for meditation. There are two periods of working meditation each day, and you're allocated your job. The type of job you get ranges from helping in the kitchen to gardening, hoovering, cleaning toilets, polishing, ironing, building, laundry, mopping, or sewing. On a retreat there are at least nine or ten periods of meditation that you're expected to attend. Each period of meditation lasts thirty-five minutes at Throssel. Some periods of meditation are double this, broken up by ten minutes of walking meditation. Scriptures are also recited in the morning, late afternoon, and after the last period of meditation. At two points in the day, you have about an hour and a half to yourself. These rest periods can be used to either rest, read, or take a walk in the monastery grounds.

The mindful spirit in which everything is done is striking. When you rise in the morning, you are expected to be silent. Everyone politely and mindfully works around each other as they use wash basins and brush their teeth. When you get a job, the monks explain what needs to be done, and then together everyone works on the task at hand. If you are given ironing as your job, there will be a specific way to do it, and you follow those instructions, doing as good a job as you can. If you're working in the kitchen, you might be tasked to wash, peel, and prepare vegetables. There will be a specific way to do this. The care and attention given to these tasks is one of the greatest Buddhist teachings I have ever received.

For example, when cutting carrots, you give the carrots a wash to take off the worst of the soil. You cut off the ends and place those in a bowl of discarded bits. You're taught that everything is precious and has a value of its own, even a carrot. You only want to cut off the ends so that you're only discarding the bits that really cannot be eaten. At home, I would cut off carrot ends that included bits that could be eaten, in a non-mindful way. You then peel the carrots mindfully, placing the peelings into the same bowl as the ends. You then cut the carrots into similar-sized chunks as shown by the monk.

You are aware of the silence in the kitchen being broken by your clumsy cutting action. Over a week, you become more mindful in your movements and begin to cut and peel in a way that is quieter. After cutting the carrots, you place them in a big sieve, washing them carefully so that every carrot is properly cleaned. Dogen in his instructions for the Zen cook talks about treating the community's food as if it is your own eyeballs. This sentiment is applied at Throssel, and every aspect of the community is treated with care, because it has a value of its own.

Vegetables are cut with this spirit, floors are mopped, altars are dusted and polished, gardens are tended, clothes are ironed and washed, and human beings treat each other in this spirit. It feels amazing to be part of this community, even briefly. Living in this way, meditating, and working with others mindfully has had a profound effect on me. Added to this is the incredibly beautiful surroundings of the monastery in the northern Pennines. Silence, beauty, and nature as far as the eye can see. I fell in love with the place and the practice. I think of the monks when I get home. I look at my watch and wonder what they are doing now; I rise in the morning and think of the monk walking around the monastery, ringing his or her bell to awaken the community.

When I leave the monastery to return home, to reenter the world,

I'm emotional. *How long have I been here? A day, a week, a year?* Time in the monastery seems to stand still. When I drive past the upper monastery grounds for the final time, I step out of the car and look across the rolling, high, barren moorland. Silence, only broken by the sound of calling red grouse. I take one long, last look down the valley, tears welling in my eyes, and take in this vista, this place I see as my second home. I look forward to these visits above everything else. I wouldn't say this out loud, but Beth knows me so well that it doesn't have to be said.

Over time, I got to know some of the monks well and developed a deep respect for them. They are human just like me, but living in the monastery for several years has brought a lightness and different quality to their being. They don't have that jaded, haggard look of someone who lives under constant pressure. It's hard to put an age on them; their faces radiate peacefulness. As I watch them going about their daily business, working and meditating, I get the sense that their practice has deepened to a level that's hard to reach as a lay Buddhist working as a CEO.

What a life, I think. At one time I couldn't think of anything better than to have the honor of living my life in the monastery, playing my part in the community; just being there and it being available to people like me, who live in the world, who come here to find peace, teaching, and comfort. I came to respect their way of life, how they lived, how they welcomed me and others into their community. But I couldn't help thinking how much I'd like to join the community, discard the world, ask the abbot to accept me as a monk, shave my head, and pull on the monk's robe.

I knew this life wasn't open to me. First, I loved Beth and the boys more than anything; I would never leave them, and this thought never crossed my mind, ever. I'm sure that had I requested to become a monk, the abbot of Throssel would quite rightly have said no and told me to go look after my family. Although I knew all of this, I still thought about monastic life daily for several years. I would be at work, sitting in a meeting, listening to colleagues complaining about something that usually wasn't that important. My mind would drift to the purposeful and peaceful life at the monastery. Something in me couldn't help but think, *I wish I were there and not here.* I would sit in meditation, and this dichotomy of feelings would surface in my thoughts regularly as I sat on my bench.

Perhaps this tension between the spiritual and worldly life has existed from the beginning. Human minds have perhaps always grappled with the question "What's the right way to live?" The Buddha found himself in such a situation. As a young man, he lived a privileged life as a wealthy prince. His father sheltered him from the harsh realities of the world and never let him leave the confines of his lavish palace. It was not until the Buddha sneaked out of his palace as a young man that he saw that life wasn't perfect.

He saw four sights that changed him forever. He saw an old man that taught him that life was impermanent and would not last forever. He met a sick man and saw that he was suffering, as was his family who worried about him. He saw a corpse, which brought home the impermanent nature of existence but also taught him how important this life is. Finally, he saw a holy man, and for the first time he realized another type of life was available and open to him. This life involved seeking a way to liberate himself from the suffering of the world. Ultimately the Buddha left his wife, Yasodhara, and young son, Rahula, to pursue the spiritual life. He would reunite with them later in his life, and they would both become practicing Buddhist disciples themselves. Did the Buddha feel the same sense of being torn between the hermit life and the worldly life as I did? Perhaps this tension is a common theme for many of us.

These thoughts surprised me. I'd never even thought of monastic life until I came to Buddhism properly in my early twenties. If I ever thought of monks, which would have been rarely, I suppose I would have pictured them as serious, out of touch with the world, offering little to modern existence. Their way of life would have seemed boring to me at one time. No alcohol. No sex. Bed at 10 p.m. Told when to rise and what to do during the day. How had I become so attracted to this way of life?

However, I had found something unexpected. Yes, the monks were committed to their way of life and to the practice. But they were neither serious nor stern. Their level of commitment was inspirational, but they were humorous, good company. They laughed at jokes and at themselves. I found they had a lightness of being where they could be present to any situation. They were kind, but this kindness was never over the top or manufactured. It was genuine. They were happy to listen to you and were open to share their view on issues and problems, without ever trying to claim their view was correct.

Their honesty surprised me as well. They didn't paint the monastery as a place of perfect peace. When I got to know a few monks quite well, they talked openly about how you could not come to a monastery to escape your problems. In fact, your problems followed you through the door. I was interested in what they had to say about this.

When you commit to and begin to live the Buddhist life and practice daily, you notice many things about yourself. Not all good. If anger is an issue for you, or laziness, it will surface in your meditation eventually, and you can't help but notice it. Buddhism encourages you to train with these facets of your personality, to sit with the aspects of yourself that you don't like. Just sit with them. Don't judge them. Let them be present, and over time, maybe weeks, years, decades, or a lifetime, they start to loosen their hold on you.

The monks told me that this was no different in the monastery. If anger is an issue for you prior to becoming a monk, it soon emerges at the monastery. The daily schedule for monks is partly designed to allow monks and laypeople to unearth their emotional baggage. A monk might be given a job they do not like, such as working in the kitchen. The abbot assigns them their job. They might really dislike working in the kitchen, but they're expected to get on with it and do their best. Unlike a job out in the world, they can't apply for another one. It might be years before they are reassigned. The meals are fantastic at Throssel because they are made with such care and effort. But there's no choice, and monks must accept what they get and try to cultivate gratefulness.

Over the years, monastic life can push people's buttons as much as life on the outside. These stories only deepened my love for Throssel and the monks; I admired their honesty and the sincerity of their lives, and the fact that they didn't hide its difficulties.

One of the many joys of staying at the monastery is access to a well-stocked Buddhist library in the lay common room. This is where I got my introduction to the hermit tradition that has long existed in Buddhism. I picked up books that inspired me and brightened my life and taught me about a way of living rarely experienced and long forgotten in the West. I read the poetry of the Japanese Zen hermit monk Ryokan and was deeply moved.

Ryokan's story is well known in Japan, and his poems are still loved in the modern day. He is sometimes referred to as the Zen fool because he lived such an eccentric and carefree life. After training for many years in a monastery, he moved to a small hut in a forest and lived there as a hermit. He would beg for his food in the local villages and became a favorite of the local children, who would all look out for him on his rounds. It was said that he was happy to stop and play games with the children without a care for what people thought.

His poems are deeply moving and describe his life living alone in his hermit's hut. Honesty shines through his poetry. He describes sitting alone at night, feeling lonely and sometimes sad, listening to the rain on his roof. He would light incense and read scriptures in the night. At other times he describes the great joy of his life, enjoying nature and taking long walks in the forests and mountains. His sincerity and commitment to Buddhist practice illuminates every word:

My house is buried in the deepest recess of the forest
Every year, ivy vines grow longer than the year before
Undisturbed by the affairs of the world I live at ease,
Woodmen's singing rarely reaching me through the trees
While the sun stays in the sky, I mend my torn clothes
And facing the moon, I read holy texts aloud to myself
Let me drop a word of advice for believers of my faith
To enjoy life's immensity, you do not need many things.

His poems describe a world of practice and beauty but still acknowledge the difficulties he faced in his life. What is it that spoke to me so profoundly? When I first read these poems, I had been practicing for two or three years. I'd already begun to experience the deep sense of peace that practice can bring, whilst still acknowledging I had areas where I was far from perfect. I'd started to slow my life down a bit and could identify with Ryokan's words encouraging us in the art of "the way" and saying we don't need many things.

In the modern world, I felt the pressure to accumulate things. There was a need to provide a home for my family and have a car to take them places on weekends and holiday. *How big does my house need to be? How much of a mortgage or rent am I willing to pay? Where do I want to live? What car should I drive? Where should we go on holiday? All our friends are going to Southern Europe; should we? Should the kids get the designer clothes they desire? Do they really need the latest computer?* My head would spin with these questions.

The tension between wanting to live as a hermit monk and my worldly life grew as I read more about the hermit tradition. Han Shan, Empty Cloud, and Bodhidharma all became my heroes whom I admired greatly. I couldn't help occasionally considering what could have been. Could I have been a monk who lived remotely, offering retreats to people who also wanted to seek the dharma? I didn't ask for or expect this tension to arise in my practice or life. It didn't overwhelm me, but it was present for many years, and I resolved to let it be there in the background but not get too involved with it. Over time, it did lessen, and eventually I came to terms with it.

What really helped me was a conversation I had with an Indian man, Sahil, I met on retreat at Throssel. We went for a walk together during a free period, and we talked about our practice. He clearly was practicing deeply and was very committed. On speaking to him, it became clear to me that he had a young family. I asked him how he managed to develop his practice whilst still being a committed parent and husband. His answer resonated with me. He said that in India there is a saying that in your twenties, thirties, and forties, you are busy with your family. You enjoy this time, doing your best to raise them and teach them right from wrong. You don't give up your spiritual life but accept it might be a bit different with a family and try your best. But once the parenthood years are over, you look forward to devoting yourself to your spiritual life, living how you want, with less emphasis on the world.

This might seem obvious to many, but this struck me between the eyes and made me think. Here I was, tearing myself down the middle, one side of my mind deeply committed to my family and life as a lay Buddhist, the other side wishing I could become a monk and eventually disappear into the mountains and live in a small hut on a mountainside or deep in a remote forest.

However, our conversation helped me realize that life is not a sprint but rather a marathon. Buddhism wasn't advising I rush through life, wishing for the family and career part to end. Life was busy just now with the children, but this would not always be the case. They would grow up and make their own way. One day there would be opportunities for me to step back from my busy life and focus more on the spiritual. Just as Dogen states in his instructions for the head cook to not disregard certain ingredients that look superficially inferior, I needed to enjoy each phase of my life, regardless of the difficulties.

Sahil's words stuck in my mind, and I was frequently aware of them when I meditated. After several years of being plagued with thoughts of becoming a monk or hermit, these thoughts began to loosen and eventually left me.

I still deeply respect the monks at Throssel and enjoy reading about the hermit way of life, but now I feel a deep contentment with my own life. This happens in Buddhist practice. Thoughts and tensions that we hold in our minds and bodies do eventually evaporate. It might take many years or decades, but if we meditate diligently and treat these feelings with compassion by letting them be there, without indulging them or berating them, they eventually release us.

I looked at the monastic life slightly differently from then on. I valued the ability to choose to do what I want when I want, like go watch a football match, go for a drink with Beth, go out for tea and stay out late, should I choose to. As a monk or hermit, I wouldn't have these choices. At last I made peace with my life in the world. I didn't have to tell Beth that these thoughts and feelings had left me; she knew.

What strange creatures we humans are, me included. Where these thoughts and strong feelings came from, I cannot say, but powerful they were. Some might say they were karmic in origin. I believe that a long and sustained meditation practice over many years helped these feelings eventually dissolve. However, my conversation with Sahil stays with me. There are still possibilities in life to live differently, and who knows what they might be and how life will develop in the future?

As I resolved these strong attachments to monastic life, I settled down into my lay life. I was never ambitious, nor did I set out to be a CEO. Doors just kept opening for me. How did this wannabe hermit end up being a CEO?

CHAPTER 5

My CEO Journey

> Confused by thoughts
>
> We experience duality in life
>
> Unencumbered by ideas
>
> The Enlightened see the one reality
>
> —*Huineng*

I was promoted to CEO at RCC in January 2013 in an unexpected and dramatic fashion after the previous CEO, Ken Morrison, died suddenly. Ken was a great guy, well liked by all the staff, including me, but on reflection he didn't look after himself well. He was a giant of a man, about six foot five, and he must've weighed well over twenty stone. He went home one Friday night in good spirits and died unexpectedly from a heart attack early Saturday morning. This was nothing short of tragic, and it came as a real shock to everyone involved with the company.

It was a strange and busy weekend for the leadership team. For some reason, Ken had written my phone number in his diary, and the police called early on Saturday morning, thinking I might have been a family member. I phoned my leadership team colleagues to let them know the sad news. We had all worried about Ken's health at times as he seemed to be putting on more and more weight and appeared breathless on occasion, but we never expected anything like this to happen.

I'd never been in a situation like this where the CEO is just suddenly no longer there. What would we do now? We agreed to meet as a leadership team for breakfast that Sunday morning, and

I volunteered to phone our chairman, Norman, to let him know what had happened. Norman couldn't make the breakfast meeting on Sunday but asked if he could meet with the leadership team for an emergency meeting at 10 a.m. on Monday instead.

The leadership team met at the Promenade Café on Aberdeen Beach. Although we ordered food, no one was really hungry. We agreed that all we could do Monday was to assemble staff first thing and tell them what had happened. To my surprise, my fellow leaders nominated me to break the news to everyone. I was touched that my colleagues were comfortable with me taking more of a lead but slightly nervous as well. I'd only been with the company for six months, less than other members of the leadership team. Graham had been with the company for twenty years, and Jason had been there four years. Despite this, they looked to me for leadership in this situation.

Monday morning came, and I arrived early, as did Graham and Jason. We operated a lot of shift working at RCC, so we'd only have a portion of our staff in the building, but we resolved to phone all other staff personally to tell them the news. We also linked up with our Dundee and Inverness staff via video link so they could hear the announcement live. Staff that came in that day were told that the company had an important message to deliver at 9:30 a.m. and it was likely the office would close for the day thereafter. Rumors flew around, but we held our nerve and waited until everyone had arrived.

I stood in front of our staff. About fifty people in all were working that morning across our three sites. "Thank you all for your patience this morning. I realize that asking you to assemble together at this time is a little unusual, but we wanted to give you this news together. It is with deep regret that I must inform you of some very sad news. On Saturday morning, our CEO, Ken Morrison, tragically passed away."

There was a collective gasp, and people began to cry and look at each other with that disbelief that only comes with the news of a death. I paused, then went on.

"The leadership team recognizes that this news comes as a great shock to us all and that we all need some time to reflect on this and process this news. We will each come to terms with it in our own way and in our own time. Therefore, the office will be closed today to all nonessential staff as a mark of respect to Ken. The leadership team will be here for the rest of the day, so if you want to hang around and speak with us or your colleagues, you are free to do so. All nonessential engagements have been cancelled today, so there is no need to worry about work."

Shutting the office was easy, but shutting our accommodation units was complicated as we had patients staying with us. With some concerted effort, we had managed to cancel meetings and other commitments that enabled most of the staff to go home.

"RCC was Ken's passion. We will make sure it survives, thrives, and continues with its good work. Today the leadership team will be meeting with our chairman, Norman Smith, to agree on the best way forward for the company over the next few months. We ask that everyone meet here tomorrow morning at 9:30 a.m., and we'll give you an update on how we intend to proceed. In the meantime, please look after yourselves and each other, and thanks for your patience and support. We'll all need each other over the coming months. Thank you, everyone."

Just a few minutes after our announcement, Norman arrived at the office for our 10 a.m. emergency meeting. Norman was a good chairman and knew a lot of the staff by first name; he first went around the office to speak to various people, which was greatly appreciated. Norman, Jason, Graham, and I made it into the boardroom by about 10:30. Norman was normally quite businesslike, but this was a unique circumstance. He spent the first ten minutes expressing his disbelief at what had happened and asking how we all were. Then we moved onto business. What were we to do?

Norman had spoken with other members of the board already. They wanted to appoint one of the current leadership team to the CEO position on an interim basis whilst the post was advertised nationally. However, they didn't want this to be acrimonious in any way as it was important for the leadership team to stick together. If none of us were willing to step into the CEO role on an interim basis, then the company would be run by the three of us as a committee, but the board would prefer to avoid this situation; they believed having an acting CEO was the best option.

Norman asked Graham first. Graham had been with the company for twenty years and was the finance manager. He was sixty-three years old and widely regarded as one of the nicest people anyone could meet. Graham was clear that he didn't want the CEO role even on an interim basis. He didn't want that kind of pressure at his age and at this stage in his career. He said he'd support whoever took on the role.

Norman then asked Jason. Jason had been with the company for about four years and was thirty-four years old. He also didn't want the job. Jason felt that he was too young, that he was still cutting his teeth as a senior manager, and though the CEO role might be something he'd aspire to later in his career, this was too early for him to take it on.

Then Norman turned his attention to me. "What about you, Hamish?" he asked. I paused before answering, and a whole host of images flashed through my mind. I saw myself standing outside the monastery, looking peaceful, enjoying a moment in the grounds. *The Buddhist CEO*, I thought to myself. How would the pressures of the job affect my Buddhist practice and family life? My family also flashed through my mind. I had a rough idea what the CEO role paid, and it was a significant jump in salary for me, more than £20,000 per year. I knew what that would mean for our family and the things that would allow us to do. It was also on an interim basis, and if I didn't like it, I could revert back to my old post. I had to take this opportunity.

I heard myself say, "Norman, I would be delighted to accept this post on an interim basis should the board wish to offer it to me." I also added, "However, I would only want to take on the role if I had the support of Graham and Jason, and if this made them feel awkward in any way, then I would respect their views and be happy to jointly run the company with them on a committee basis."

With relief in their voices, both Graham and Jason stated that they would support me and appreciated me putting myself forward. So it was decided quickly that I would become the interim CEO of RCC. The board agreed to my appointment, and the following day I had a letter confirming this. I moved into Ken's former office and started what was to become an enlightening but difficult journey.

That evening, I drove home with very mixed emotions. On the one hand I felt excited about what had happened, but I also felt sad about Ken, and uneasy that this opportunity had only come about through Ken's death. I could almost hear him saying, "Hamish, just bloody get on with it" in his very direct manner and thick Cockney accent.

I had a small Buddha statue in my car as a reminder to practice mindfulness when driving and attempt to be a compassionate and considerate driver; I find it too easy to get frustrated on the road. Today I looked at the peaceful image of the Buddha and tried to focus on the moment—to just drive, enjoy the drive, and let thoughts come and go. My mind raced. *What will Beth say when I get home? Will I be a successful CEO? What will it really be like? How much pressure will come with it? Will I cope with the pressure?*

When I arrived home, Beth and the boys had prepared my favorite tea for me. They knew I'd had a difficult day, and they wanted me to come home to a great welcome and my favorite food. I gave Beth a huge kiss and hug and thanked my sons. My plate was full of rice and a beautiful homemade egg curry, one of my favorite Indian dishes. In the center of the table sat a range of accompaniments: popadom, naan bread, spicy onions, mango chutney, and a selection of vegetarian bhajis and samosa. I was delighted. It's a special thing to feel the love of your family.

I poured myself some orange juice and broke off a piece of popadom, smothered it in mango chutney and spicy onions, and sat for a minute or so, just crunching away and enjoying the delicious taste. I felt tension rising in me, and a need to tell Beth and the boys what had happened. Beth looked concerned, and the boys intrigued.

I glanced up at them and said, "Well, guys, believe it or not, you are looking at the current interim chief executive of Rural Cancer Care." They gasped, and Beth rose and hugged me while the boys offered congratulations. I thanked them all, and then Beth said, "Let Dad finish his tea, and we'll go and make him a coffee, and then I'm sure he will come through to the living room and tell us every detail of his day." I nodded, appreciating Beth for creating this little moment of space for me to assimilate and process. She knew me better than I knew myself.

After I finished my meal, I made my way through to the living room. I sat in my chair, and Beth came through with my coffee and chocolate biscuit. I really was spoiled. This was a bit of an evening ritual for me. I would come home and usually meditate and either make tea for everyone and then eat or, if Beth was home first, eat what she'd made for us. Once I had my tea, I liked to have a cup of coffee and a chocolate biscuit and hear from everyone how their day had been.

Now comfortable in my chair, I saw from their eager faces that they wanted to hear all about my day. I spent the next hour or so telling them about what had happened and answering their many questions.

It was interesting to see their different reactions. The boys were chuffed for me, and at fifteen years old, they thought it was cool that their dad was a CEO. But Beth clearly felt torn. She was delighted for me and expressed how much I deserved it for all the hard work I had put in throughout my career. Still, she worried about the stress and what that would do to my health and wellbeing. She did like the fact that it was on an interim basis as I could always go back to my other job if I felt it was too stressful. She always backed me.

It was now 7:30 p.m. and time for evening meditation. I made an offering of incense, sat on my meditation bench, and meditated for thirty minutes, trying not to focus on anything, just trying to be present, accepting that thoughts come and go.

That evening my meditation was neither calm nor peaceful. Even Fudge appeared restless. A line from Dogen's "Rules for Meditation" kept popping into my mind: "You should meditate in a quiet room, eat and drink moderately, cut all ties, give up everything, think of neither good nor evil, consider neither right nor wrong."

I also thought of a conversation I was fortunate to have with a Zen master, Reverend Daizui Macphillamy. He was a hero of mine due to the fact he'd been the chaplain, or right-hand man, to my Zen heroine Reverend Master Jiyu Kennet. During this conversation he said that all he hoped for in regard to his legacy was that his fellow human beings might say that he'd been a half-decent human being. Both Dogen and Daizui suggested that what is important is to live a simple and humble life. I too wanted to live a simple and humble life, but now I was about to become a CEO. *Is the role of CEO compatible with Buddhist life?* I pondered this as I tried to meditate.

Think of the good I could do, though, said another voice in my head. *The company can become an exemplar in how to treat and engage staff, and if I can improve our service delivery, we can reach out and help more people.* My mind raced on like this until the bell sounded to signal the end of my meditation. I bowed and sat for a few more minutes, with trusty Fudge still at my side, enjoying the peace of the room, both of us more settled. The candle illuminated my Buddhist altar, and the shadow of the Buddha danced across the wall. Incense now filled the room, and for a few moments I touched on something which all meditators or people with a deep spiritual or religious practice experience from time to time. The connection didn't last long, but I felt it and I appreciated that moment. I stood and bowed to my bench and to the altar and left my Zendo for the first time as a CEO.

The next few months flew past. I settled into the CEO role, and trying to keep the company going after Ken's sudden passing felt exciting. By the time the position was advertised, I was enjoying the job so much that I naturally decided to put my hat in the ring and apply for the post on a permanent basis. I attended the interview in the spring. The board had clearly been impressed with how I'd coped during my interim appointment and how I handled myself at the interview, and from a group of thirty applicants, I got the job. I was now officially the Buddhist CEO—thrilling, scary, and still slightly surreal.

Two months in, the interim role had shown me very clearly that there was a lot to do and the company faced many challenges. I liked Ken, and he'd done a lot for the company, but like any company, there's always room for improvement. Our finances were precarious. We had suffered significant losses of about £100,000 per year over the last two years, something that couldn't continue. The only reason we'd survived was because we'd built up healthy cash reserves during good times. I recognized, as did Norman and the board of directors, that we had to stop losing money if we were going to survive. Norman told me when I was promoted, "This isn't your mess, but it's your job to sort it."

As well, the services we were commissioned to deliver weren't delivering nearly as well as they should. They did help people and could be quite effective for the customers we dealt with, but they fell well short of the expectations of the organizations that funded us. Of particular concern was that we couldn't always demonstrate effectively what we did to help our customers. We needed to evidence our social impact much more.

Other major issues were our workplace culture and general poor staff morale. Staff weren't highly engaged with the company, and they voiced that they often felt neglected. Adding to this feeling was the fact that there had been virtually no investment in the company infrastructure for years. The IT systems barely worked, the phones were dated and terrible, there were no HR systems nor policies of any kind, and the company structure was such that only the CEO could make big decisions, which held up the most basic decisions and procedures, causing great frustration amongst staff.

So, in my first year and a half as CEO, I set about trying to fix these issues. I felt really motivated and excited about the challenges. The board seemed supportive, as were my leadership team and middle management team. Staff were eager for change, and I tried to include them as much as I could in the change process. There were a few doom merchants who resisted changes, but they were a small minority, and I was determined not to let them get in the way of progress.

In terms of my Buddhist practice, I continued to question whether becoming the CEO was the right thing to do. I'd read many Buddhist books and heard Buddhist monks caution about being ambitious. It worried me that this could detract from the joy I felt as a Buddhist practitioner. I worried that the stress and difficult decisions I would inevitably have to make might change me. However, Buddhist teaching talks about training being possible under any circumstance. It is my practice that is important, and how I choose to live my life, and this should not be dictated by external factors. If I could help create a compassionate but ambitious culture, our staff could enjoy their work and life far better than at present. I took up the role believing I could deeply practice Buddhism whilst still fulfilling the role.

The first three years felt like one success after another. In my first year, I stopped the terrible financial losses the company had experienced. I turned a loss of £117,000 in the previous year into a small surplus of £7,000. I was particularly proud of the fact that I did this without anyone losing their job, by introducing more robust financial processes. RCC hadn't been financially maximizing the contracts we already had, and from then on I ensured that we claimed and drew down every penny that was due to us.

It also became clear that we were paying for a lot of things we didn't need, such as IT support contracts and external services like health and safety and HR. It seemed like we didn't get much for our money, so we stopped many of these contracts and dealt with these things in-house. With a more sensible approach to how we drew down money, and by being careful what we spent our money on, I was soon able to bring some control to our finances. On top of this, I instigated a new fundraising strategy. Historically RCC hadn't raised much money through donations but rather earned its money mainly through delivering contracts. I brought in a small fundraising team, and within three years they were taking in close to a million pounds through corporate sponsorship, endowments, and our new annual dinner.

Our staff knew that we were a charity, and they didn't expect to be lavished with gold, but they did, quite rightly, expect things to function and to feel appreciated. Two things that really drove our staff crazy were the company vehicles and our IT facilities. In my first month, I reviewed both. It was clear that our vehicles were old, bashed on the outside, and untidy on the inside. Our IT wasn't fit for purpose, so I initiated a major upgrade of both, resulting in the delivery of brand-new vehicles and a modern IT system that actually worked. The immediate effect was that staff could see things changing. They were being listened to, and this raised morale. I set up transforming our services and made sure I engaged staff in the process. This motivated people more and led to huge changes in how we delivered several of our services.

Over the space of two years, RCC experienced many transformations, and our services went from barely hitting their key targets to being high achieving. All our partners, which were predominantly national and local governments and lottery funding, could also see the huge changes taking place. Our funders were delighted, and the profile and reputation of the organization rose significantly. Because we were now trusted to deliver, we began to win new contracts and additional work. We also used the money raised through our fundraising team to deliver new services that were often shaped by frontline staff, further boosting morale. Most importantly for me, our efficient service delivery meant we now worked with and supported far more cancer patients year on year, and this made me extremely happy. Our customer satisfaction scores went through the roof, and everyone at RCC was infected with excitement about what we were doing and could finally see the impact and value of our work.

I wanted to put the company out there and gain recognition for what we had achieved, so we entered several high-profile awards. We even entered the prestigious *Sunday Times* Top 100 Companies awards, not thinking for a minute that we'd make the list.

On entering, all our staff were sent a detailed questionnaire asking them about their views on the company's leadership, management, their team, how the company supported their wellbeing and development, and how they felt about their terms and conditions of employment. Staff completed the questionnaire anonymously, so they could be as honest as they liked. We would receive detailed feedback on the anonymous responses, and if nothing else, gathering this evidence would be a great way to learn and improve. We entered for the first time in 2013. Much to my surprise, we made it into the top 100 in our first year and then went on to achieve top 100 for the next seven years in a row.

All of these developments gave me heart that we were doing something right. I couldn't help wondering if having a Buddhist CEO at the helm, someone genuinely trying to treat staff and customers with compassion, was having an effect. We also won other awards locally and were even recognized as employer of the year within the care sector. We won an award for our efforts to improve our employees' mental and physical wellbeing, which gave me huge personal satisfaction.

Although I was excited, I did begin to have concerns for my health. A few unexplained health issues had cropped up since I had become the CEO—silly little things I brushed aside, like my fingertips occasionally going numb. Sometimes they got so sore I found it hard to button my shirt in the morning. They would stay sore for a week or two, then crack and peel. I didn't mind too much, but it wasn't a great look at meetings. I felt self-conscious about it. Thankfully, they healed quite quickly, and would look normal again within a week or so—only for them to do the same again a month or two later. This happened regularly over a five- or six-year period.

It eventually worried me to the point that I went to the doctor to find out what was causing this. I tried numerous creams, but nothing worked. The GP said it was nothing to worry about, so I put it to the back of my mind.

Spiritually, I still managed to keep up my daily practice. I meditated every morning and recited scriptures and always tried to take their teachings into my daily life. I tried to be mindful, be present in each moment as much as I could, and before any decision I took as CEO, I would ask myself, *Is my decision compatible with Buddhism?* My philosophy was to treat others with compassion. I learned quickly that this didn't mean my compassion would be reciprocated, but I like the Zen saying "Expect nothing." And that's what I did. I tried to never expect anything from others and to make sure my actions matched my philosophy and values.

I was aware on other levels that being a CEO did detract from my Buddhist practice in some ways. It didn't matter how much I tried: I was always thinking about the job. When meditating, my mind was busier and less peaceful, full of chatter, and would often replay events from work. I felt a different level of tension in my body.

Beth noticed it too. She felt I was less responsive to her and not as much fun. She would point out that I held my shoulders higher and I looked tense. I had to admit this was true; I felt the tightness in my muscles at times. I didn't like this, but I had to accept this was how it was for me in this moment, in my mind and body.

Despite this, on balance I enjoyed the experience during the first three years. Having more disposable income improved our family life, and I felt I'd managed to take my Buddhist principles into the job, which helped me enormously in the role. Things were going well, and this CEO seemed to be doing okay.

Until things started to change. About three years into the job, I realized just how lonely and stressful this job could be. Smooth seas, as they say, never make good sailors, and I was coasting head-on into the eye of the storm.

CHAPTER 6

Steven & Co

The night is fresh and cool

Staff in hand, I walk through the gate.

Wisteria and ivy grow together
along the winding mountain path;

Birds sing quietly in their nests
and a monkey howls nearby.

As I reach a high peak a village appears in the distance.

The old pines are full of poems;

I bend down for a drink of pure spring water.

There is a gentle breeze,
and the round moon hangs overhead.

Standing by a deserted building,

I pretend to be a crane softly
floating among the clouds.

—Ryokan

Elaine wasn't the first major staffing challenge I encountered on my CEO journey. Other issues really tested me. The first three years had been so positive. I was highly motivated and felt like the sky was the limit. From a Buddhist perspective, my biggest challenge was staying humble and keeping my feet on the ground and trying not to get caught up in ideas of success. This was all about to change, and the following years proved challenging in ways I hadn't expected.

Let me tell you about Steven. Steven had worked at RCC for two years when I joined the company in 2012. He'd led a team of about fifteen cancer support workers, who primarily coordinate people's stays with us, making sure the clients are cared for and appointments are arranged and professionally managed. He managed this team well, and under his leadership they had greatly improved their performance and level of customer service. This was impressive because the staff team had quite a few difficult characters with strong personalities, but Steven handled them skillfully, and I was impressed.

When Ken died suddenly and I was promoted, it left a few vacancies below me. I'd been the operations manager at the time, and there was an assistant operational manager below me. We advertised these posts, but in the meantime, I needed to fill them on an interim basis. At the time I promoted Elaine to operational manager and Steven to assistant operations manager. This gave me a chance to observe them both in action. We received several applications for the operational manager post; both Elaine and Steven applied, and we interviewed four external candidates.

By the time the interview came around, I'd been able to observe Elaine and Steven in their interim roles for six weeks. Elaine's shortcomings have been discussed, but even at this point, she had not greatly impressed me and at times annoyed me. She found a problem in everything. Instead of making things work and finding solutions, she got bogged down in minutia and couldn't see the bigger picture. Early on, I could tell that if she oversaw our operations, they would stagnate, and perhaps even go backwards. She certainly wasn't the dynamic leader we needed.

Steven, on the other hand, threw himself into his role, and in six weeks it was clear he was making a difference. He changed some of the processes our staff followed, freeing up their time to spend with customers and allowing them to be more efficient and effective. This had a positive impact on our performance statistics, especially customer satisfaction, which was important to me. Unlike Elaine, Steven naturally found ways to make improvements. He was a positive and dynamic leader who could drive change and quickly understood the improvements needed.

The interview day arrived. Norman and another board member, Margaret Donald, joined me on the interview panel. As I expected, Steven was by far the best candidate on the day. He sold himself creatively, and his passion and desire for the job shone through. Elaine gave a sound but scripted presentation followed by her answering interview questions in a manner that was far from inspirational. I decided to appoint Steven to the post with the backing of Norman and Margaret.

Steven was thirty-four, young for such a senior post, but his performance as a team leader over several years, and what he showed he could do during his six weeks in the interim position, convinced me he could do the job well. This felt like a big call, as Elaine thought she was the favorite for this post, and I'm sure most of my colleagues would have felt the same way. But even they couldn't deny Steven grabbed hold of this post with impressive enthusiasm and vigor.

Once appointed, he repaired any damage done to his relationship with Elaine and went on to build a successful partnership with her. He then set about tackling some of the performance issues that plagued the main service he oversaw. Although I'd only been at RCC for about nine months at this point, I could see that some of our services needed overhauling. Staff were stuck in a rut and didn't have a clear idea on how to improve the service, and there was a sense of malaise about the whole company that needed to change.

Steven threw himself into the job wholeheartedly. Very quickly he set new individual targets for the staff and built in much more concentrated, regular, one-to-one support for all the staff through their team leaders. Steven conducted a staff skills audit and identified weaknesses in their knowledge and set about providing training in the areas where they needed support. Service targets were shared monthly with the staff, and when a target was achieved, it was celebrated in some way. Sometimes this was as simple as ordering in a nice lunch for staff or coffee and a cake being delivered to their desks from the local Costa Coffee shop. This, mixed with some of the ideas I was implementing as CEO, quickly saw staff morale rise and lifted these services out of stagnation.

We had to meet with various representatives from our funders on a quarterly basis to review the performance of the services they funded. Our main funders were the UK government, the Scottish government, the Big Lottery Fund, and local authorities. These meetings had historically been quite painful for RCC due to us being so far off the mark in our performance. The KPIs set for our services were challenging, but it was not unusual for us to be somewhere between 25 percent and 40 percent off target on most KPIs come the end of the year, which is not great by anyone's standard.

When I gave Steven the job, I explained that this had to change, and I would give him all the support I could to help him achieve this. I wanted to change this first and foremost for my own pride. I didn't like the idea of being connected to services that didn't perform well, and this service wasn't anywhere near where it needed to be. I also didn't like the idea of RCC providing any poor services. It wasn't the image I wanted to present. How could we win new contracts to provide more services when our current services were performing so poorly?

Steven was the man for the job. He relished the challenge, and within six months of being in post, there were tangible improvements in performance. Something significant had happened, and Steven could, quite rightly, take the credit for it.

But something happened. After Steven had been in this post for a year, he started to change. I'm not sure why. It started when we met to discuss an upcoming meeting, and he seemed irritated and frustrated with me. It was nothing over the top, but I'd never experienced Steven like this. The meeting passed, and we agreed upon an outcome, but I remember thinking that it was odd. A few weeks passed, and I noticed more changes in his behavior. He was short with me at our leadership team meetings, and the way he spoke to me in front of other team leaders left me slightly uncomfortable. These changes were subtle at first, so subtle that I wondered if I was imagining them. After a few weeks of reflection, I decided I wasn't imagining anything. We had a scheduled one-on-one meeting coming up, and I decided to raise the issue with him then.

I held these meetings with all my leadership team members periodically. It was a chance for me to hear what was happening and offer them support and guidance. Steven entered the room, and from the beginning, he seemed defensive. His body language was closed, his arms folded, and his tone slightly aggressive.

Steven was about six feet tall, blue eyes, and had a serious look about him. He kept himself fit, so was muscular and slim. I always felt he showed his emotions on his face, and when he was annoyed, he just couldn't hide it. He was neat in appearance, clean shaven, and his hair was short and neatly combed, and he normally wore smart shoes and trousers with a shirt open at the neck.

Arms still folded, he gave short, one-word answers to my questions. Irritated by this, I told him I'd detected a change in his attitude of late and asked if there was anything wrong or if I had done anything to upset him. "No," he replied, but then he paused and after a while said that he was just frustrated at the pace of change within the organization and he felt I could have made some decisions quicker than I had. He went on to explain that he would have liked the marketing and communication manager post that we'd just created to have been agreed on earlier. I asked him to explain.

"You know that marketing my services has been an issue, and it just doesn't feel right that myself and the team have to create our own marketing materials. That has put a lot of pressure on me lately. I shouldn't have had to put up with that. It took ages for you and the board to make a decision to give the new post the go-ahead, so I wasn't impressed. I just don't think this was fair at all."

I was quite surprised by this, but I welcomed open discussions with senior staff and was pleased to finally get what was bothering him out in the open. I explained that I was slightly disappointed that this was his view, but I wanted to explain and hopefully help him to understand my thinking. Establishing this post hadn't been an easy decision, and I needed to have the board's support. The timing was tricky because when I initially considered creating the post, RCC was only just beginning to make a small financial surplus. The board, although pleased to see us making a surplus, was still nervous after the heavy losses sustained prior to my appointment. Although I'd demonstrated two years of sound financial stewardship, they were anxious not to see the company slip into financial difficulty again.

We had started the financial year in the red, but thankfully that was only a temporary position, and we bounced back into the black later that year. I didn't feel it was the right time to approach the board about introducing a new senior post. I waited until the end of the financial year before asking the board to support me, and I believed that I had been right to do this. Reaching the end of the financial year in surplus meant the board really started to trust me and my ability to control the company's finances. I reminded Steven that he should feel proud and supported by the fact that we had now created and appointed Leona to this post and that it was he who had been instrumental in this. He had put forward a good business case for the post. I thought that this would have pleased him. It showed the influence he had over big decisions in the company. But this didn't seem to make any impact.

He sat there stony faced, arms folded, like a young child. I was annoyed by his response. I decided to take another approach. "Steven, I'm really disappointed with your reaction towards me today. I've tried to be fair and give insight into my thinking about why I made the decisions I did. My hope was that you would see this as a fair response from me, but your body language and sharp, dismissive tone suggests otherwise. Whatever your view, I need to say something important to you. It's vitally important that you and I can work together for the sake of RCC. We don't have to like each other, but we do have to get on and be able to work constructively with one another. It's my expectation that we are civil to each other and that we can have professional conversations where we can agree and disagree without falling out. I do expect you to be constructive when we speak and for you not to be dismissive."

I watched him closely as I spoke, and I sensed his fury growing. He found it difficult to give me eye contact, and his arms remained folded. All he could say was "Okay, Hamish, let's just move on and work together as best we can." I saw no point in continuing the meeting, so we ended it there. I hoped that this would act as a shot across his bow and maybe bring him to his senses, but my hopes were proved wrong. Very wrong.

Several months before this conversation with Steven, following Graham's retirement, we recruited a new finance manager, Sheena Baxter. Sheena was a qualified accountant with plenty of relevant experience. She had worked for several large corporate companies in the private sector, and this was her first job for a charity.

Soon after Sheena started working with RCC, it became clear that she was hardworking and enthusiastic. She was focused on her role and did it diligently, but she kept her head down and didn't always make time to get to know her colleagues. This could sometimes rub people up the wrong way. The charity sector, in my experience, attracts people who are outgoing and very people centered. These people value their colleagues and like to get to know them well. Sheena didn't really get involved with this. Overall, though, I was very pleased with her contribution to RCC. She was excellent at her job, and if she was a little quiet, then so be it.

Sheena started with us in October 2015, which was about the same time I noticed changes in Steven's attitude. I don't think the change was linked to Sheena, Steven was not exactly being warm towards his new colleague. I never saw Steven act rudely towards her, but there was no doubt he was challenging to work with.

Steven began to raise concerns about Sheena with me. He would complain that she was aloof, didn't work closely with him or other members of the leadership team. I would point out to Steven that as senior leaders it was our responsibility to get to know Sheena and constructively challenge her where necessary, but we also had a duty to try and forge a strong and constructive professional relationship with her. I also pointed out that I had observed him being abrasive towards Sheena at times, which maybe didn't help the situation, and encouraged him to give Sheena a chance and try to constructively engage with her.

Over the next few months, Steven's attitude continued. In fact, it became worse. He started to withhold information from me. Normally, each month he would provide me with a report on his service's performance, but these stopped. I had to ask him for this information, and he was often subtly rude when I asked for it.

Other strange things began to happen. Steven shared an office with two other members of our leadership team: Jason, our sustainability and partnership manager, and Leona, our marketing and communications manager. Jason had been with the company six years now, and Leona for only six months. Jason was a mild-mannered gentleman who worked hard, and I'd always got on well with him. He was a committed family man with four young children, and was liked by all his colleagues. Leona was married and in her late twenties with one daughter. She was glamorous, fashionable, and always immaculately presented. I never disliked Leona; I found her hard to get to know and never quite connected with her, but she had been hardworking and committed to RCC, and her colleagues seemed to like her.

A few weeks after the changes in Steven's attitude, I noticed a difference in Jason and Leona too. It was far more subtle than Steven's sudden change, but it was obvious to me that they had been talking. I wasn't surprised by Leona, as she seemed to follow Steven's every word, but I was at Jason. He was clever, bright, hardworking, and very much his own man. I thought he would be a positive force and encourage Steven to at least be professional. However, it became clear that divisions were occurring; he sided with Steven and Leona, and together they formed a powerful clique. They talked amongst themselves, supported one another, and grew hostile towards me and, to a lesser degree, Sheena. Our leadership team meetings became frosty and unproductive, and for a short while I was at a loss for what to do.

As well as this, a situation arose with Norman. He asked if I could find a work placement within the company for one of his friend's sons. Board members of charities aren't supposed to use their position for any personal gain or favor, but this was a seemingly reasonable request. I knew Norman well enough to know his intention was only good. It wasn't as though he was asking me to give someone paid employment.

I raised this at my leadership team meeting, expecting support to find a placement. But I was met with hostility from Steven, Leona, and Jason. They argued we shouldn't be tolerating this type of request from the chairman or any board member and I should refuse it. I was slightly taken aback; the level of enmity seemed over the top, but at the same time, there was a process to follow, and perhaps they were right. Norman shouldn't have asked to bypass this.

It is a cliché to say that the CEO role is a lonely one, but that night I felt it. The job was hard enough, but to suddenly find your leadership team were against you and for it to happen so suddenly was a shock. In the first three years of my journey, I had made some tough decisions and faced my share of difficulties, but this felt different. For the first time, I wasn't sure what to do.

I decided that trying to keep my leadership team together was more important than worrying about Norman's friend's son. I wanted to help Norman, but this felt like a test. I would either be seen as weak by my team or I had to let our chairman down. The next day, I emailed Norman, telling him there was no openings for placements at this time and it might be some time before one becomes available. His reply was curt and to the point. He was clearly disappointed, and he asked to see me in person to discuss the issue further. Over the next few days, whilst waiting to meet with Norman, the frosty reception from my colleagues continued. I was confused, angry, and lost, so I turned to my soul mate, Beth. What did she make of it all?

Beth and I sat down together in our living room, both with a cup of tea, and told the kids not to disturb us. Beth knew this was serious as I rarely spoke to her about work. I explained the situation to her, telling her about the dynamics within my leadership team and Norman's request and his subsequent response.

The first thing she did was get up and give me a hug. "That sounds awful, Hamish. I can't believe you're being treated this way." Beth said it seemed they were displaying bullying behavior towards Sheena and me, and that I should seek support from the board. She was disappointed that of all times when I needed my chairman, Norman was instead annoyed for not doing his friend a favor. "You've always valued and respected Norman, though, and although this is unfortunate, I'm sure he'll get over this quickly, especially when he realizes the dynamic you're facing within your leadership team."

Her response let me know that I was on the right track; I wasn't wrong in feeling this situation was unusual and serious. I chatted through with Beth what I intended to do. My plan was to meet with Steven and tell him again, but more assertively this time, that his behavior was unacceptable and that I expected to see changes quickly. I was also going to meet with Sheena to see how she was feeling and make sure she had the support she needed. The situation with Norman was merely an annoyance, a blip, and I just had to see how that unfolded. I really needed his advice and support with this situation, but instead he was in a huff.

One word that Beth used stuck in my mind: *bullying*. This was an area Beth knew a lot about. She had been a workplace culture champion in a previous role and knew all too well the signs of bullying and undermining behavior. I also knew Beth was very perceptive, a good judge of character, and if she thought I was being bullied, it was worth thinking about. She gave me some information to read so I could do my own research.

I was shocked at what I found. There's a ton of literature out there about this subject, and there is general agreement on what the main signs of workplace bullying are: belittling and embarrassing colleagues in front of others; withholding information from someone; manipulation, especially in the form of being nice to some colleagues and excluding others; lying; and unreasonable behavior. When I read this, it hit me like a train. This was exactly what Steven was doing to me, and I feared he was doing the same to Sheena. He had belittled me in front of my colleagues, he was clearly withholding information from me, I felt he was manipulating Jason and Leona, befriending them and trying to turn them against me, and his behavior at times was unreasonable. I was in no doubt that he was trying to bully me, and there was no way I was going to let him succeed.

While meditating that evening, my mind was very restless. *I am the CEO; surely nobody can bully me. What does this say about me? Does it mean I am a poor leader? How do I pull this back? Do I have the skills to pull it back?* Meditation was like this for a few weeks as I grappled with a deep unease.

My Buddhist practice helped me greatly at this time, an anchor in the storm. There is nothing in Buddhism that says a practitioner must be a doormat. Yes, we train and practice "the way" to develop wisdom and compassion and to help all living things, but sometimes standing up for what's right is the wise action to take. I wanted to act from a place of compassion and a willingness to do the right thing, but I would come out fighting on the front foot for the best outcome in this situation. This toxicity was not going to continue on my watch.

The next day, I asked Sheena for a meeting. She came into my room and sat opposite me at my meeting table. "This is very mysterious, a meeting with the CEO with no detail on what we are to be discussing," said Sheena, laughing nervously.

"Nothing to worry about," I said. "I just want to talk through some issues I've observed within the leadership team." I asked her how she found working at RCC and if she felt supported by her colleagues.

I immediately knew I'd hit a nerve. Sheena tried to speak but then bent her head forward and began to sob. She desperately tried to speak through the tears, but it was incoherent, so I calmly told her to take her time. Whatever Sheena was feeling, it was clearly deep rooted and traumatic. After about ten minutes, tears were still flowing, but she had regained enough composure to speak.

"I just can't take it anymore. I feel that I'm trying my best to be polite and civil to Steven, but every time I do, it's just thrown back in my face. I ask him for information so that I can assist him with his budgets and forecasts, and he says he will give the financial information by a certain date. Then that date passes, and I must go to his office and ask again. Then he always makes some sort of snide remark in front of Leona and Jason. It just makes me feel small, stupid, and extremely frustrated. I now dread coming into work; I hate the atmosphere within the leadership team. I fear Steven, and sometimes I am physically sick before coming into the office. When I see Steven, I become nervous and anxious and can feel myself beginning to sweat. I have not slept well for a couple of months now. When I wake in the night, I'm often thinking about him and how much I dread seeing him the next day.

"Steven seems to have influence over Leona and Jason," she continued, "and they do not speak to me either now. Leona is outwardly hostile and is often just silent around me. Jason, who I once thought was a lovely guy, seems to be enthralled by Steven and listens to his every word. I fear for my job as I know how these things work. The bully is always protected, and the person who raises the issue is usually made to leave, and I know this is what will happen now."

I was shocked and deeply saddened that a member of staff under my watch was feeling this miserable about working at RCC. I was furious with myself for not seeing this earlier, and at Steven for his outrageous behavior, but first I needed to make sure Sheena felt supported. I knew that everything she had just told me was true. Everything she had described I'd noticed myself.

I told Sheena that I was appalled that she had been made to feel this way, that I believed what she had told me about Steven's behavior, and that this would not be tolerated at RCC. Bullying was a form of behavior that I detested. The organization would stand with her and would resolve this situation.

We spoke about how we should proceed. Sheena was not sure she wanted to formally raise the issue. I asked her why, but it was clear she was fearful of the repercussions across the leadership team. I explained that I was going to challenge Steven about his behavior and that I would drop into this conversation that I was concerned he was treating others inappropriately, too. Though I was not completely comfortable with this approach, there was some merit in seeing if Steven would change his behavior before taking formal action against him. I made clear to Sheena that if Steven didn't change his behavior, I would have to escalate what she had just told me about how he made her feel.

Steven was out of the office a lot that week, visiting our Inverness and Dundee offices, so I penciled in a meeting for the following week. However, matters escalated quickly, and Steven and I soon found ourselves at loggerheads once again.

Steven and Leona were interviewing for a new team leader post at our Inverness service. This post was funded through a local authority, and as was usual practice, someone from the local authority sat on the interview panel, a man called Archie Henderson. I'd met Archie before. He'd been involved in funding some of our services for several years, and I'd always found him easy to work with. I never gave the interviews much thought before as Steven and Leona were more than capable of handling this.

On the day of the interviews, I was still in the office when my phone rang at about 5:45 p.m. It was Steven, and he sounded very angry. He caught me off guard, and I had to say, "Steven, please slow down and start again. I have no idea what you're talking about."

"Hamish, you are not going to believe what just happened. We were interviewing all day, and we had five candidates in total. As usual we scored all the candidates on their presentation and how they answered each interview question, and it came down to a final two. Leona and I scored the same person as the highest scorer, but Archie had that person in second place and had scored another candidate higher.

"We discussed this amicably, but Archie felt very strongly that the person we scored highest was not right for the job. After a while I said, 'Archie, I hear what you're saying, but it is two against one here, and because Leona and I prefer the other candidate, we'll appoint that person.' But then Archie said that the contract we have with them clearly states that the council officer designated as overseeing that contract can veto any appointment to the post of team leader. Is this true, Hamish? If it is, it's a bloody disgrace. Who the fuck is Archie to tell me who the fuck I appoint as my fucking team leader?"

I was quite taken aback by Steven's language but could also appreciate that this was a very unusual situation that would have frustrated me as well, although not to the same degree. Concerned that Steven might have displayed his anger towards Archie, I asked him how he'd left it.

"I kept my cool in front of Archie and said that I will check the contract and perhaps we should all just sleep on it and speak again tomorrow, to which Archie agreed."

I was reassured by this, but I reminded Steven of the need to remain professional. The local authority in Inverness has been good to us over the years, so I didn't want to spoil our relationship with them. I tried to calm the situation and said, "Steven, I can hear you're upset by this, which I can understand, but Archie is usually a reasonable guy. Let me check the contract tonight and let's you and I speak in the morning."

Steven didn't sound overly pleased with my response, but he

muttered under his breath that he agreed, and we'd speak in the morning.

We kept our contracts electronically, so I looked it up after I put the phone down. As was the norm with these contracts, it was long, and it took me a while to find what I was looking for. There it was, in clause 15.3: "The council retains the right to veto the appointment of the service's team leader post should the appointed council officer deem that the suggested candidate is not capable of fulfilling the role as required in the job description. The designated council officer's decision will be final on this matter."

I had never realized that this was in the contract. It seemed to be a very unfortunate clause and not one that engendered trust or partnership. Whatever I thought, it was clear that Archie had the right to veto our preferred candidate if he chose to do so. This was not going to please Steven. I closed the computer and locked up the office and headed home.

Early the next morning, I arrived in the office and made myself a cup of tea. I was at my desk by 8:30. The phone rang almost immediately as I sat down. It was Steven, and he still sounded angry. I confirmed that I had checked the contract and there was a clause that stated that Archie had the authority to veto our appointment.

Steven went off. "Why on earth did you sign that contract with that clause in it? This demeans RCC as an organization." I let him vent for a few moments before closing him down.

"Steven, this contract was signed before my appointment, and I don't appreciate your tone. I am telling you please to calm down and listen to me. The contract is clear, and no amount of shouting or complaining is going to change that now. I need you to accept that and concentrate on using your skills to try to persuade Archie that your preferred candidate is the person for the job. If you cannot negotiate with him, then you must accept his decision.

"Whatever happens, RCC needs to maintain good relations with the council, and don't forget that this is a fantastic service that we will be delivering and it will allow RCC to help many people living remotely in the Highlands to access cancer treatment in Inverness. You should not lose sight of that."

Steven could tell by my tone that this was my final word. He mumbled, "Okay" and ended the call by hanging up.

His behavior had been disrespectful and condescending. My ego felt bruised. *Am I being too sensitive here?* I wondered. No, my intuition was warning me that this was further evidence of Steven's bullying behavior; he had overstepped the mark again.

Steven went back to Archie, and it became clear that Archie was not going to change his mind. Steven and Leona had no choice but to appoint Archie's preferred candidate to the post. When I saw them both back in the office, they were still furious about this decision and annoyed that I allowed it to happen. Their reaction seemed extreme to me, even though I could understand why this was frustrating. I reflected upon this and concluded that this situation could happen again. I agreed that this clause in the contract wasn't helpful. I wondered, too, if Archie had found yesterday stressful, having to argue his case with Steven and Leona.

My Buddhist practice has taught me that it is better to find positive and skillful solutions to situations like these. I didn't like the idea of a contractual rule having the potential to damage relationships. We deal with people suffering from cancer, and it is crucial RCC get these appointments right. Ideally, they would be chosen by RCC managers in partnership with the funding body, but if there is a dispute about who to appoint, I believe the final say should sit with RCC. I resolved to try to do something about this, but I was going to tackle this behind the scenes and not let Steven or Leona know; I feared it would only fuel their negativity towards me, the council, and Archie.

I spoke to the director of health and social care at the council, a gentleman called Noel Strachan, whom I got on well with. Ultimately, Noel had responsibility for overseeing RCC's contract with the council, and he delegated this to Archie. I spoke to Noel's secretary and arranged a call with him for early the following week. I called him, and after sharing pleasantries, I explained why I had called.

I relayed the story of Archie and Steven disagreeing over whom to appoint to the post. I made clear that I was not complaining about Archie and that the council had a contractual right to take this course of action. Then I explained that I worried that this could impact the level of service we give to our customers and impact the relationship between RCC and council staff. I proposed that for this reason, we change this part of the contract moving forward; if this situation arose again, then RCC as the employing agency should have the final say on an appointment.

Noel listened closely and could see my point of view. This had been raised before by another organization, but nothing was changed at the time. Noel said he wanted to speak to his colleagues in contracts and procurement first and then get back to me. What he was sure about, though, was that even if he agreed to change this clause in the contract, it would take time and would not be done in time to alter present circumstances.

The day before my meeting with Steven where I was going to tell him how disappointed and worried I had become about his behavior while outlining the changes I needed to see, I got an unexpected call from Norman asking if he could see me. This was unusual. He didn't often just phone up and ask to see me.

Norman arrived later that day and made his way up to my office. I got him a cup of tea, and we chatted for a few minutes about everyday things. Then he said, "I've something I need to raise with you, Hamish." I sat back and listened to Norman tell an interesting tale.

He explained that Steven had approached him and our vice chair, Angela Black, last week to raise his concerns about me. Steven was disappointed in how I handled the situation with Archie and made RCC look weak. He said that this came on the back of other decisions that were either made too slowly or were not in the interest of RCC. Norman said that Steven had taken him by surprise. He was annoyed that Steven had gone behind my back, but at the time he merely told Steven he would need to think about the issues he raised.

Norman later spoke to Angela, and she felt the same way; both were concerned by Steven's actions and wanted to raise it with me directly and get my take on things. I explained to Norman that the Archie situation had been unfortunate, but I was working behind the scenes to see if we could address that clause in the contract going forward. I went on to say that Steven had grown very negative and had formed a clique with Leona and Jason, who were making life difficult for myself and Sheena.

Norman was furious that Steven had been acting this way and asked why I hadn't mentioned it before. I told him honestly that I felt things were a bit frosty between us, and I hadn't had a proper chance to chat this through with him. Norman didn't respond to what I said directly, but he nodded and said, "Okay, Hamish, I hear you. But let's get our heads together to sort this. How should we proceed?"

The CEO in me wanted Steven to be disciplined and even dismissed for going behind my back like this. How could I trust him again? The Buddhist in me thought, *Hang on a minute; is this compassionate, wise action? Probably not.*

Steven was talented, had sorted out some failing services for RCC, and was capable of really good work. For whatever reason, he had displayed bullying and other negative behaviors that were not acceptable, and they needed to be addressed directly. But Steven had earned the right to rectify this situation.

I talked this through with Norman, and he said he wouldn't blame me for wanting Steven to be dismissed. However, we agreed that he and Angela would meet Steven later today, and they would tell him they were disappointed in him coming to them with matters he should have discussed with me first, they were aware of his inappropriate behavior towards me and others, and it was not going to be tolerated by RCC. They had considered disciplinary action against him, but in recognition of his impressive work history at RCC, they were giving him the chance to go to mediation with me. This would be conducted by an external company with the aim of resolving our differences and finding a way in which we could work together constructively.

Norman phoned me after their meeting with Steven, who was left in no doubt about how they felt about the situation and that they expected more from a senior member of staff. They had called his bluff. Norman said that he looked shell shocked but agreed to attend mediation with me. Norman asked if I could set up the mediation and keep him in the loop.

The first thing I did was let Sheena know that things were being dealt with. I couldn't disclose exactly what was happening, but I said that Steven and I were meeting next week to resolve our differences and that the board was aware and fully backing me. Sheena was relieved to hear that Steven was being challenged about his behavior, but she was still nervous. She asked if she could work from home for a few days, to which I agreed.

Later that day, I spoke with HR and told Morag about what had happened and how I planned to proceed. Although we had our own HR resource in Morag, I felt it would be inappropriate for her to conduct the mediation and that we needed to look for an external resource. We had used an external HR company, Black & Mathers, occasionally for training and for second opinions when needed. I contacted them to find out if they could support us with the planned mediation.

Sandra Styles was the owner. I'd known her for a few years and got on well with her. I began to explain the situation, leaving out Steven's name. She listened patiently, and when I finished speaking, she said, "I know who you're speaking about. It's Steven, I bet."

"What made you suspect I was talking about Steven?"

Susan replied, "You'll remember, Hamish, that it was Steven that introduced us a few years back, and I have attended a few meetings at RCC where Steven has been present. I've also bumped into him at networking events. Every time I've met Steven, I've come away from the meeting thinking that I wouldn't like to be on the wrong side of him."

Sandra's comments were the first external feedback I'd received on Steven. I'd been sitting in meetings with him, thinking but not certain his behavior was over the top and unnecessary. But clearly others had noticed it as well. Sandra thought Norman's plan to attempt mediation in the first instance was a good idea, and they had a highly trained member of staff, Thomas Farquhar, who she thought would be ideal for the job in hand.

That evening at home, I sat to meditate with Fudge at my side, and my mind was restless. The most intrusive thoughts were about how I had handled this situation or let it arise in the first place. *Am I to blame? What does this say about me as a CEO and leader? Could I have intervened earlier? Did I promote Steven too early in his career and he just wasn't ready yet? Is my leadership style too relaxed? What will the board think about this?*

As a Buddhist, I practice to release the grip of the self, but that night I was aware of the self more than ever, and the ideas I had about myself weren't helping me approach this situation. These ideas are a smoke screen masking the true, deeper reality of life.

After meditating, I offered merit to those I knew were suffering in their lives, and then I did something I hadn't done before. I made myself a cup of tea and came back into the Zendo and just sat on my bench in front of the Buddha. The room was silent, and Fudge slept at my feet. The candle flickered slightly, illuminating the Buddha's peaceful face and casting his shadow against the wall as the sweet smell of incense permeated the room. I stayed there for what must have been an hour, soaking in the serenity and beauty of the moment.

The mediation had been scheduled for Tuesday the following week. Thomas from Black & Mathers arranged everything and phoned Steven and I separately to let us know how the process would work. Thomas also phoned Norman to talk him through the process and also to remind him that he would not be privy to any of what was said during the mediation. What Norman would be privy to was the action plan that we hoped myself and Steven would work out between ourselves, with the expert help of Thomas.

Tuesday arrived, and I turned up at Black & Mathers' offices, ready to begin. The mediation lasted three hours. Initially Steven and I were in different rooms and Thomas shuttled back and forth between us, clarifying the situation and where disagreements had arisen. Before long, all of us were in the same room. I sat and listened to Steven as he laid out why he had been so frustrated with me. It boiled down to what he felt was the lack of change in the organization and my inability to stick up for RCC and tell other organizations what we were doing rather than give into them all the time.

I then got my chance to say that I felt the pace of change had been fast and reminded Steven of RCC's vastly improved financial position, workplace culture, service performance, customer satisfaction, and our improved infrastructure. I went on to explain that I believed it was important to be seen as a constructive organization and one that tried to solve problems for and with our funders, and not be an organization that is antagonistic, which would work against us in the long term.

After that, I was able to address Steven's behavior towards me. I explained why this was unhelpful in creating a dynamic and supportive culture amongst our leadership team and why I needed it to stop. If it didn't stop, then I couldn't see how our leadership team could become effective at driving forward the ideas and changes RCC needed to be successful.

By the end of the mediation, we had agreed an action plan. Steven agreed to address his behavior towards both Sheena and me whilst being more respectful of the decisions I made. For the next six weeks, we would meet each week for thirty minutes to openly put on the table any issues between us and seek a positive resolution.

I was pleased with how the mediation went, and Steven had fully engaged with the process. He had heard my explanations for certain decisions and timeframes that had frustrated him. I hoped this would allow him to see that decision-making can be incredibly complex and sometimes the CEO is juggling a range of competing demands that he might not be aware of. We shook hands at the end of it all. This was to be the start of a new and improved relationship between us.

Over the next few days, the positive atmosphere in the office was obvious. It was clear Steven was making great efforts to get along with me. I observed a positive change in how he spoke to and dealt with Sheena. Later in the week, Sheena shared with me that he was like a new man and that she looked forward to coming into work again.

Steven and I had the first of our weekly meetings. We spent thirty minutes having an open discussion about work and our interactions. The idea was that we could explore any areas of disagreement or confusion and stop them from becoming issues that caused friction between us. We met over the next four weeks, and Steven asked me quite a few questions about decisions I had made, and we had a good chat around them. It seemed like he saw where I was coming from. My hope was restored. The situation had been turned around in a positive way. I came to look forward to our meetings.

In the fifth week, he knocked and entered the room as usual. Immediately I sensed something was up. He wore an expression that I had come to recognize as a warning sign. It was subtle, but he just could not hide when he was angry and annoyed. I hoped I was wrong.

"Steven, nice to meet with you again. I believe this is our fifth since mediation. I hope you've been finding these meetings as useful as I have. Any questions you'd like to ask or anything you want me to clarify? How has work been for you this week?"

I was met with a stony silence. Arms folded, Steven looked out of the office window. I didn't jump to fill the silence. I could tell that Steven was thinking deeply about what to say next—and that it was not going to be positive.

"Hamish, this whole thing is a bloody joke, to be honest. Us meeting like this is so false. And as far as I am concerned, I have never treated Sheena differently from anyone else. I'm just not comfortable with this at all. As for the mediation, what else was I to do but go along with it on the day?"

I've seen and heard a lot that has surprised me in my time as CEO. Sometimes the way people react in a situation can be incredible, but this moment topped them all, and my jaw dropped. It was as if time stood still, and in that moment, something clicked. I wasn't dealing with a normal, rational person here. I was dealing with an out-and-out bully.

It took all my strength and skill to hide these thoughts from showing on my face and in my body language. I paused for a while, thinking how to respond. There was tension in the room; Steven had declared war and was clearly up for the fight.

"I have to say, Steven, I'm surprised by your reaction. I have observed your behavior towards me and Sheena these past few weeks and had thought you were making such a commendable effort to get along with us both in a way that is constructive, positive, and in step with what we agreed during mediation. To be honest, I have quite admired the strides you have made since the mediation to repair relationships. I had been thinking this was a credit to you, and I know that Sheena feels the same. But are you telling me now that you don't feel the same way?"

"That is exactly what I'm saying, Hamish. I didn't have much of a choice, did I? If I did not participate in this bloody mediation, Norman said there would be an investigation, so I felt that I had to go along with it. I feel angry that you and Sheena have put me through this, and I still don't agree with many of your decisions and never will. And I've never been discourteous towards Sheena, by the way. I think this whole charade is a joke."

Steven was clearly enjoying telling me what he thought and displayed an arrogance and disdain that I didn't appreciate. For a moment, I saw myself sitting in the Zendo with the lights off and only the delicate flame of a candle lighting my altar, the Buddha sitting silently, his shadow dancing across the wall amidst the smell of incense. This prompted a sudden thought of the ninth Bodhisattva precept: do not indulge anger. I returned to my senses. I was a Buddhist practitioner, attempting to follow the Buddhist way. I was facing someone seething with anger and hatred. My instinct told me this needed to be dealt with swiftly, but I needed time to reflect. I wanted to respond to Steven as another human being and not face anger with anger.

"Steven, thanks for your honesty. I am stopping our meeting now, and I am going to think through what you have just said and its implications and how I want to proceed with this matter."

At that point I thanked him for his time, stood up, and walked out of my office and headed downstairs. As I stood, I caught sight of Steven's face, and he looked surprised, as if he had not expected me to react like that.

My head was reeling, and since it was a beautiful, sunny day, I took a walk to help clear my thoughts. I tried to walk mindfully, my attention on every step, the movement of my body, and my breath coming in and out. I tried to be mindful for fifteen minutes or so before even attempting to think through what had just happened and how to respond.

When I considered what Steven had said, I felt a deep sense of clarity. I had acted very fairly towards him in the face of his continual rudeness and obstructiveness, but he had just crossed a line from which there was no coming back. There were no doubts. If I didn't act now, I knew how this would play out. Eventually relationships in the leadership team would break down. When this happened, Steven would let slip to Sheena that he had told me that he did not believe in the mediation process right from the beginning. This would lead to distrust between Sheena and me. Steven would then have succeeded in turning the whole leadership team against me.

I was not going to allow this to happen, and this was the week to strike back and regain control. I knew not to react that very day; it's easy to overreact when emotions are high. I cleared my diary for the rest of the day and the next so I could think through how to deal with this.

I reached my decision quickly. I was going to tell Sheena what Steven had said. I couldn't have her believing that Steven was fully engaging with the mediation process and that his friendly behavior towards her was earnest when I knew that Steven harbored ill will towards us both. I would allow Sheena to work from home until this situation was sorted. I would speak to Norman and tell him that I could no longer work with Steven and that I was asking for his support to find a way to move him out of the company. Steven was poisoning people against me and acting as a block to change. RCC was never going to thrive until he was gone.

I phoned Norman and told him about what Steven had said during our meeting. He wasn't totally surprised. Neither Norman nor Angela had been impressed with the way Steven approached them recently. Others on the board were aware that the mediation process had taken place and were concerned about the difficulties within our leadership team. All experienced leaders, our board members knew that an unhappy leadership team did not bode well for any company. They were supportive of me, and when I'd told Norman a few months back about Steven's change in attitude, he shared his own thoughts on the matter.

Norman had observed Steven being unnecessarily abrasive and rude towards me in front of others. Several board members had approached him over the last few months to say that they had noticed similar behavior. In addition, Norman had noticed the negative clique formed by Steven, Leona, and Jason.

Norman was an old hand at these situations, and he played his cards wisely. He also was not vindictive. He saw a young talented man who he hoped could learn from this experience and use it to become a better person and a better professional. Steven had to leave RCC, but Norman wanted to give him the chance to leave with dignity if possible.

I liked this approach; it felt very Buddhist, and I like to think I would have acted in a similar way had the decision fallen to me. The situation had become so toxic that there was no coming back from it now. Norman was experienced in these matters. He had a private meeting with Steven and explained that his behavior had become intolerable. Norman suggested that he might want to consider moving on from RCC in a manner of his choosing and which would not damage his career going forward. Should he leave now, RCC would agree to pay him a reasonable sum of money and to supply him with a favorable reference.

Steven went home that evening and thought about Norman's offer, and the next day he accepted. I was relieved. The alternative would be to sack him for bullying and insubordination. This way allowed him to move forward without the black mark of a dismissal on his employment record while allowing RCC to also move on.

On Friday, an email drafted jointly by Steven and Norman was sent to all staff. It stated that Steven had been offered another job and because he had been asked to begin immediately, RCC had honored this and he would be leaving now rather than serving his three months' notice. The email also thanked Steven for his long and good service to RCC. Some staff saw through this, I'm sure, but it allowed the whole sorry episode to be closed off. For most of us.

Leona took the news of Steven's departure badly. I found it surprising that a leader could expect any CEO worth their salt to allow a member of staff to behave so negatively towards them. Even Susan at Black & Mathers and the RCC board members, who weren't in the offices regularly, picked up signs of Steven's destructive and toxic behaviors. Leona must have witnessed his unacceptable behavior on multiple occasions. Did she think this was okay?

She took sick leave for some weeks, then departed RCC the following month to take up another post. Although she was hardworking, I met her departure with relief. She was part of Steven's clique, and I wanted his influence gone from RCC altogether.

I was more concerned with Jason's reaction. I rated him highly both professionally and personally, admired his work ethic, and he was always caring and considerate towards his colleagues. After Steven's departure, we had a heated argument about what had happened. Jason was angry Steven had been asked to leave. Our cross words cleared the air, and we agreed we had to move on in order to work together. We did this for another year and a half before Jason took up a post with another company. He left on good terms and keeps in contact regularly to see how we all are.

There were still a few challenging characters at RCC. That is just life in a workplace. But when people become toxic and begin to influence others, it changes team dynamics and impacts negatively on the whole culture of an organization. Although managing diverse teams of people can be difficult, if they work hard, embody the company's values, act respectfully towards me and other members of staff, and don't undermine or bully others, this is a good baseline to work with.

This horrible period lasted several months; then I went straight into the situation with Elaine, which dragged on for about a year by the time we got to the tribunal. I didn't enjoy one single moment of these situations, but looking back, I know I would make the same decisions again.

As CEO I did my best for RCC, and once we got rid of Steven, the company went from strength to strength. We won even more work contracts and funding bids, and staff morale increased dramatically, customer satisfaction improved, we earned more money than ever, and our services performed better too. Like a bottle of champagne, I had loosened RCC's cork and let out all the pressure, and it breathed a sigh of relief. Had I not acted decisively, I would still be a hostage to Steven and his whims. I would still be attending leadership team meetings with stony, hostile faces glaring back at me. That just could not go on. Sheena thankfully got herself back on track and greatly appreciated the support Norman and I had given her. She went on to thrive in her position for the next few years.

These tribulations, however, took their toll on me. The excitement I felt during the first three years of my CEO journey had vanished, and I felt battle weary. In those first few years, it felt like I was walking on air. Every day brought excitement and new challenges. I was so proud of turning the company around from the failings of the past. I could see the difference I was making—developing people, improving the culture—and got so much satisfaction from the difference RCC made to society, helping people in need who really benefited from the support we gave them during their treatment.

But these staffing issues sapped my energy, and I don't think I ever fully got back to where I was. Throughout the Steven and Elaine situations, my fingertips got worse. I pushed it to one side as I was so busy, but they were becoming sore more regularly, peeling on and off throughout that time. Other little niggles cropped up, strange things began to happen, and I wondered if my health was failing.

"Jason," I shouted through to his office, "are you ready to leave now?" We were due in Dundee for a meeting in an hour that could result in a lucrative new contract.

We took my car and headed off. It was a crisp, clear day, and the sun was shining in my eyes, so I didn't notice at first the orange flicker in my left eye. I put my sunglasses on and blinked a few times. It got worse, so I rubbed my eye, hoping it would just go away, but the colors seemed to spread, and my vision became kaleidoscopic. I felt fine, but although the colors were beautiful, it wasn't conducive to safe driving, so I pulled off the road as soon as I could. Jason was concerned about me and wondered if we should turn back. But because the meeting was so important, we pressed on. I managed to get through the meeting without anyone knowing about my psychedelic ocular experience.

Beth said I should go to the doctor, so I got an appointment the following day. He sent me to an optician, who said I'd suffered an auricular migraine and it was nothing to worry about. Some people get them regularly, whilst others may only experience them once in their life. I hoped that it was a one-off, and I was relieved it wasn't something more serious, like a stroke.

I carried on as normal, but a few months after the ocular experience, the left side of my face became numb whilst I was sitting at my desk one day. At first, I wondered if I was imagining it, but the numbness spread and started to affect the skin around my lips. I went to the bathroom to look in the mirror. My face looked normal. No redness or swelling. Over the next hour the numbness spread across the whole left side of my face, from the bottom of my chin to the top of my forehead. Quite scared, I phoned my doctor, who told me to come to the surgery immediately.

The doctor checked me out and concluded that there was nothing seriously wrong with me. Predicting that the numbness would slowly disappear, he advised me to go home for the day and rest and see how things were in the morning. Although I was heartened that nothing was seriously wrong, I was still concerned. The doctor said that they saw a lot of patients with unusual symptoms like this that were not easily explained. Usually the symptoms went away and never came back. He reassured me that all the tests he conducted gave him full confidence that I was not having a stroke or a heart attack. He did say to come back if my face was still numb the next day.

I took his advice and went home and rested. As the day progressed, my face slowly regained sensation. By the time I awoke in the morning, I felt normal, but Beth and the boys were worried about me. Beth thought it was the pressure of the job and asked me to be careful and honest about my health if things got worse.

The following month, another strange episode occurred. When dressing one morning for work, the left side of my body was sore. The pain steadily grew worse over the next few days. Three strange lumps appeared directly where the soreness had developed, as if someone had laid three short lengths of string just under my skin at equal distances apart. They felt coiled, soft, squidgy, and sore to touch.

I immediately feared the worst. *Do I have cancer?* I made an appointment with the doctor again. She examined me and said she was certain that they were not cancer, but she was puzzled as to what they actually were. She wondered if they were an atypical presentation of shingles, so I was given medication for this. The medication made me feel horrible, but I took it anyway. It had no effect on the lumps. They remained on my body for about nine weeks, and then they disappeared, seeming to heal up slowly of their own accord. The doctors never got to the bottom of what had caused them.

I've been fit all my life and have never been one to worry about my health. But this series of strange health symptoms began to plague my mind. What were they, and why couldn't the doctors tell me what was causing them? My instinct told me something was wrong, but I didn't know what, and work was busy, so I pushed these things to the back of my mind as best I could.

Every day I got up, went to work, dealt with things, came home. The shine had come off the CEO role, and the shock and negativity of Steven, Elaine, and the leadership team had taken its toll. I began to wonder if being a CEO was for me after all. During my meditations, I thought regularly of the monks at Throssel Hole. Their lives seemed idyllic, far removed from employment tribunals and the daily grind of people working against me. I would think about some of my Zen heroes, Jiyu Kennet and Empty Cloud, and the Zen poets Ryokan and Hanshan. They all had lived quiet lives, not seeking money, fame, or glory.

I yearned at times for a simpler life. How on earth had this wannabe monk become a CEO? Was this job destroying me from the inside out? I didn't know, but for the first time in a while, I felt unsettled and ill at ease. Meditation was difficult now, but I kept going with my practice and was still grateful for it.

It was interesting to see just how much RCC progressed once Steven and Elaine were out of the picture. It was a real lesson for me on my leadership journey. Toxic people can cripple a CEO and the company's performance, and you must tackle them head-on if you and the company are to survive and thrive. Everyone should be given a chance to change, but if they don't come on board with you, then they must go.

During all these challenges, I looked forward to my visits to Throssel more than anything else. They grounded me and brought me back to myself. The peacefulness and sincerity of the place reminded me of what is profoundly important in life: to live a life of practice, be present, live each moment as best I could, and show compassion and respect for all beings.

I still cried when I left Throssel at the end of each retreat. I followed the same routine each time I left. I drove along the bottom road to the T-junction and took a left over the high road to Hexham. As I passed the upper slopes of the monastery's grounds, I would stop the car and get out. It was always quiet, not another car or person in sight. I would look down into the monastery grounds, tears often rolling down my cheeks, the buildings and the monks that mean so much to me hidden from view by trees. I would stand and stare at this oasis of peace for ten minutes at least before I tore myself away, driving slowly until I reached Hexham, desperately trying not to leave Throssel country too soon.

And then there was Fudge, who blessed me with one final lesson. Fudge was fourteen and had been showing signs of old age and deterioration for some months. He loved to run and go on long walks, but his walks had started to become shorter until, one day, he stopped running. Over the summer, walks became slower, and he began lagging behind, one of his back legs trailing slightly. The vet said he was in pain, but not too much, and he suggested Fudge could still enjoy life for a few months yet.

But one morning, when I got up early to meditate, I went down to see Fudge and found that he had lost control of his bowels during the night and the room where he slept was a mess. He looked at me with a stare I will never forget; it just said, "I'm done."

He was in pain that morning, it was clear, so I cleaned him up as gently as I could and made him comfortable as I cleaned the room. I knew what had to be done. Beth and the boys came down to see what was going on, and we all knew this was the end. It was a painful morning with everyone spending tearful last moments with our great dog. The boys had grown up with him so didn't know life without him. Beth adored him, and he had been my meditation companion for many a year. How I would miss his head resting on my lap.

All things are of course impermanent, but this felt hard, really hard. Beth and the boys could not face taking him to the vet, so I took him. I could hardly speak when I arrived, but the vet and his staff dealt with me and Fudge with a compassion and skill that I will never forget. I held him close to me as life slipped from him. Fudge, the greatest dog ever, was gone.

By the time autumn arrived, I felt lackluster, tired, and my body was stiff and sore. I slogged through my workdays and missed Fudge more than I thought possible. I needed to see my beloved Throssel once more. I needed it to nourish my mind, body, and practice.

CHAPTER 7

Segaki

> Breathing in, breathing out
>
> Moving forward, moving back,
>
> Living, dying, coming, going—
>
> Like two arrows meeting in flight,
>
> In the midst of nothingness
>
> Is the road that goes directly
>
> to my true home.
>
> —*Gesshu Soko*

Seven years into my CEO journey, I felt jaded. Despite making positive changes to the company, on every level I felt underappreciated and frustrated.

Those staffing issues never seemed to end. I was continually disappointed and surprised by senior and junior colleagues' conduct and behavior. Is it too much to expect people to be positive and kind to each other? I began to think it was. Did I really want to do this anymore?

I hadn't felt this burnt out before. I needed a break and some inspiration. I looked at my holiday calendar and could see I still had a lot of holidays to take. I knew what I needed to do, and that was to head to my spiritual home, Throssel Hole. I checked their website to see if they were hosting any organized retreats in October, and thankfully they were holding a weeklong retreat called *segaki*. I had always wanted to attend segaki, although I had never made it down in the twenty years I'd been practicing. But this was going to be the year.

Segaki is a Japanese word that means "feeding the hungry ghosts." In Buddhism, hungry ghosts can mean a few things. Gakis are often depicted in Buddhist imagery of the six realms as beings with large bellies and long, thin snouts for mouths. It is said that these beings died in confusion, and although they are hungry for the truth and for peace, they cannot consume the dharma or any form of sustenance due to their long, thin snouts. The snouts represent their ignorance and lack of understanding of how to nourish themselves spiritually. Because of this, they cannot hear or understand true spiritual teaching, and they remain hungry and confused.

The gaki, as well as representing a being who has died in confusion, can also represent confusion in this life. Sometimes we try to consume experiences or material objects, but no matter how much we consume, we never seem to satisfy our hunger for peace and contentment. With the way I was feeling about work, I could certainly identify with a gaki.

I phoned the monastery and spoke with the guest department, who gave me more details about the retreat. Essentially it was going to be sesshin, intensive meditation, focusing on our thoughts and feelings about death, culminating in a beautiful ceremony for the hungry ghosts. I signed up there and then, and I only had four weeks to wait.

I needed silence and peace. I finished work on Wednesday, which gave me a couple of days to relax and to spend time with Beth before I headed for the sesshin. Saturday soon arrived, and it was time to leave. Beth got up early with me, and we ate a cooked breakfast together before I departed. Beth kissed me goodbye.

"You deserve this retreat, Hamish; you really do. Make the most of it."

I always feel a bit awkward heading off to Throssel on my own without Beth, but she makes it easy. She knows how much the place means to me.

I left at 9 a.m. on the Saturday and drove slowly and mindfully down the A90, heading for Edinburgh, which marked the halfway point on my journey. From Edinburgh I headed for Jedburgh in the Scottish Borders. I stopped at the town of Lauder, about twenty-five miles south of Edinburgh, and took part in what has become an Aberdeen meditation group tradition. This tradition was started by one of our long-standing members, Martin McLean. Everyone stops for a break on their way to Throssel at the Flat Cat Gallery in Lauder. Martin told me this before I first traveled down to Throssel, and I've kept the tradition ever since.

The Flat Cat serves up beautiful food. Its walls are adorned with art from local artists, much of which depicts landscapes and birds, which I love. I sat by the window and let the world drift by for thirty minutes or so. I felt my CEO life slowly dropping away and Throssel's presence drawing ever closer. It sometimes felt like Throssel called out to me, as if it knew when I needed to go. I felt it calling once again.

After finishing my lunch, I browsed through the shop, and my eyes were drawn to a necklace—a silver chain with a circular pendant, which had an intricate tree in the center of it. I was sure Beth would like it.

It had taken me about two hours and forty-five minutes to drive to Lauder, and I had about as long still to go. I enjoyed the drive through the Borders and then headed into Northumberland in Northern England. The North of England has a unique beauty. The mountains are not as high, wild, or rugged as Scotland's, but those rolling, undulating, heather- and fern-covered hills, barren and foreboding, welcomed me.

I arrived at 3 p.m. after about six hours driving and was met by Reverend Claire and Reverend Hubert. They both gave me a warm welcome, and it felt great to be back in the presence of the monks once again. After exchanging pleasantries, I was shown to my room and told that the retreat would start with a medicine meal at 6 p.m., and I had free time until then.

Most trainees sleep in the meditation hall, but there are about twenty rooms for guests as well. I had felt so tired and drained that I asked the monks if I could have a room to myself.

The room was small with a single bed, wardrobe, small chest of drawers, table with chair, a kettle, and a selection of tea bags. There was a simple white cup and a comfy chair by the window. The Zen tradition emphasizes keeping life minimal. This room was comfortable, tidy, and warm, but it was certainly humble and austere by modern Western standards.

In the far corner was a small altar with a statue of the great and compassionate Bodhisattva Avalokiteshvara. This Bodhisattva is often depicted in female form and stands in her robes, holding a water vase from which she pours forth the waters of compassion on all beings that call for her help. There was also a candle, water bowl, and an artificial plant. The candle illuminates the altar and signifies the light of the Buddhist teachings, the water bowl signifies the purity of the teachings, and the plant represents all living things. I used the matches on the bedside cabinet to light the candle and bowed to the altar, making an offering of the candle to the Bodhisattva. It is said that Avalokiteshvara is the bodhisattva of great compassion who hears the suffering and cries of the world. I asked her to hear my cries and to help me find peace this week.

I then decided to go for a walk in the monastery grounds. Throssel sits on a very steep slope with a spread of about 500 feet of elevation between the bottom of their grounds to the top. I walked slowly up to the very top where I found a stone seat, and although it was cold, I sat for thirty minutes and took it all in. The roofs of the various monastery buildings protruded from the tall trees below, and all around were the rolling hills of the Pennines. There was no wind, and the world was quiet, not a sound.

Quite unexpectedly, a tear rolled down my cheek. I let the tears flow for a minute or two. Enjoying the moment, the peace, I sensed that I felt ready to let go of something. I had a strong impression that Fudge was with me. *Is he one of the reasons for me coming to segaki?* I wondered.

I'm not one to get too excited by tales of mystical experiences, but meditating for twenty-plus years has taught me that occasionally strange things do happen. Amongst other strange incidents, I've had moments of release where it feels that something heavy has left me. Discussing these with the monks, I was always told that they'd had similar encounters, but the key was to just be in the moment with them and move on and not get caught up; this would only encourage clinging to the experience.

However, one other meditation experience that stuck out for me over the years also related to Fudge.

My parents brought my brother and I up to have a deep respect and love of nature. We were an outdoors family, always hiking in the hills and fishing as children. We spent family holidays in Assynt, in the Northwest Highlands of Scotland, where we would camp or caravan in far-flung, remote places like Achiltibuie and Clachtoll. I developed a deep love of nature as a child, and today I still hike and birdwatch. My dad and grandpa were both peaceful men who respected nature deeply, but interestingly, they both had a strong dislike of dogs. As I grew older, this seemed rather incongruous to me. Why did they dislike dogs so much when they were such nature and animal lovers?

This dislike of dogs had passed to me. When Beth first met me, she was amazed at how dogs reacted to me when we walked together. I could be minding my own business in the park, and a dog would run up to me out of nowhere and start barking aggressively. I was never outwardly cruel or hurtful to dogs; I just didn't like them, and somehow, they knew.

A few months after I began meditating seriously, I started seeing an image of a dog in my mind, feeling its presence when I meditated. At first, I thought it was my mind playing tricks on me. But the dog remained present for several years, and I realized that I wasn't imagining this; the dog was trying to tell me something. One day I told Beth that I felt we were meant to have a dog. She was, of course, surprised to hear me of all people say I wanted a dog.

Eventually the kids reached a certain age where they too started to ask for one. Beth had grown up with dogs and was keen to get one. We discovered that a local farm bred pedigree working cocker spaniels, and we were fortunate enough to be given the first choice from a recent litter.

One dog stood out to us all. There was this beautiful, dark-brown puppy sitting in the middle of his four siblings, who were all black with a little white. I knelt and lifted him out of the litter and held him up so Beth and the boys could see him. He was ridiculously cute. On closer inspection we could see that he was not completely brown; he had white on his chest and a small white patch on his nose. The boys looked at him, delight in their eyes, and said in unison, "I want that one." Beth and I both smiled; it was decided. This little dog was going to become the latest member of our family. We had to wait a few weeks to pick him up, but it was not long before we took him home. We all fell in love with this beautiful creature, and the boys named him Fudge. They were eleven when we got him.

Fudge became the center of many of our weekends. The working cocker spaniel is bred to be a gun dog spending long days out in the hills, so it is hardy and full of stamina and energy. Fudge certainly fit the bill and liked nothing better than to go on long walks. The longer, the better. We took him up hills and mountains and marveled at his energy as he sped off like lightning to chase after birds and rabbits. We would slowly plod up the mountain, and he would run ahead of us, and when he noticed how far behind we were, he would run back down to us before running up ahead again. I am sure he sometimes climbed the mountain the equivalent of three times. He never seemed to tire, and we all loved his company. He rarely barked, was great with strangers, and was very obedient. He would sit, lie down, roll over, and stop when commanded. He was simply the perfect dog.

My relationship with dogs changed instantly. When I walked Fudge, other dogs didn't look at me anymore. When I was out walking on my own and came upon a dog, they didn't bark at me or act aggressively. At the same time, dogs stopped appearing in my meditation. I can't explain this rationally; it was like something had left me, and I had a strong intuition that I'd cleansed a karmic inheritance related to dogs. I wanted to find out more about why my dad and grandpa had developed this dislike of dogs in the first place.

I asked my dad about the origin of this aversion, especially considering his clear love for Fudge. He explained that he'd never really thought about it before but that his dad had always been very wary and dismissive of dogs. I asked why, and my dad suggested that I speak to my grandma about it. My grandfather had died six years before we got Fudge, but my grandma was still alive and in good health. Though I often went round to see her, I hadn't been in months; work got in the way. But today I wanted to ask about my grandfather.

I was always slightly nervous speaking to her about my grandpa, in case it upset her. They'd been deeply in love and enjoyed a sixty-year marriage together, and she still missed him deeply. When I arrived at her house and rang the bell, I was met by a beaming smile and a huge hug and kiss on the cheek. This was a smile that I'd loved all my life, and I still delighted in being in her presence.

She was small, about five foot two, and very thin but not frail. Her dark hair was permed and always looked immaculate, as did her clothes. She wore a distinctive pair of black, thick-framed glasses. Her beaming face was kind and friendly, and a youthfulness shone through her sparking blue eyes. As I expected, a plate of cakes and biscuits awaited me, and she shuffled off into the kitchen and came back into the room with a pot of tea, which would be served in fine china cups. We sat sipping our tea, and she asked me how I was getting on, how Beth and the boys were, and how work was going. I helped myself to a piece of her homemade carrot cake. She'd made it especially for me; she knew it was my favorite, and it was to die for! Once she'd finished telling me all her news, she asked, "But what brings you round, Hamish? I haven't seen you in a while."

"This might seem like a strange question, but I've been wondering about why me, Dad, and Grandpa all have, or in my case had, a dislike of dogs."

My grandma looked a bit surprised, and I could tell she was intrigued. "My goodness, Hamish, what on earth got you thinking about that?" she laughed.

I explained my story about the dog appearing in meditation and how dogs used to act aggressively towards me and how this had stopped now that I had my own dog.

My grandma knew that I was a Buddhist, and she was quite supportive of this. She had her own Christian faith but was interested in any story that had a spiritual dimension. Grandma went to see psychics regularly with her friends, and she would often tell me about spirits who had contacted her through mediums and the messages they'd relayed. She was fascinated with my theory about some sort of karmic link between me, Dad, Grandpa, and dogs. I explained that when we got Fudge, it was almost like this link was cleansed, and whatever this thing was with dogs, I had let go of it for good. Did she know why Grandpa had such a dislike for dogs?

"Ah yes, now, that's true. Your grandpa did not like dogs. Now I hear you say it out loud, I suppose it does seem odd."

Her smile extended at the edges as she thought of the man she loved, but there was also sadness in her eyes. "He loved birds, just like you. He could name them all, and he loved plants and trees, and he would have walked in the hills every day of his life had he not had to work." She took a deep breath. "But I think I can enlighten you as to where this dislike of dogs came from." I sat upright, eager to hear the story she was about to tell.

"You know your grandpa George fought in the Second World War and he served as a solider in the Gordon Highlanders regiment?" I nodded. "Well, he fought in a famous and terrible battle at St. Valery in Northern France in 1940. It was a terrible and brutal battle that he rarely spoke of." Her voice broke as she recalled these events, and a tear ran down her cheek. She touched my hand and smiled. "Hamish,

I want to tell you this story as it makes me proud of him. He came through a lot, and I admire him for it. War is upsetting, but that doesn't mean we shouldn't speak about it."

I sat back and listened.

"He went off to join the army at age nineteen. He had no choice; all able-bodied men were conscripted."

"How did he feel about that? It must have been awful," I said.

"It was a strange time for us both. We had only met about a year before, in the summer of 1938, and we fell deeply in love and were having the time of our lives. Like all young couples, we just wanted to be together all the time and went to the cinema together, dancing, and went out cycling and for long walks. Life seemed wonderful, but then there was talk of war with Hitler." Her voice broke again, and tears flowed down her cheeks. She paused for a moment. "I haven't talked about these things for some time, Hamish. It's amazing how strong the memories still are. I remember those days as if they only happened yesterday."

She continued, "I remember when Chamberlain, the British prime minister, announced to the nation that we were entering war against Hitler. I sat round the radio with my family, listening intently, and my heart sank when I heard Chamberlain say that all able-bodied men between the age of eighteen and forty-one were to be conscripted into the army within the next few months. I thought of George and wondered how he was feeling about the news. We met later that evening and cried together at the thought of being parted."

My poor grandma was truly upset now, and I felt uncomfortable, so I offered to make tea. As I made a pot, Grandma dried her eyes and visited the bathroom. I felt awful for putting her through this, but she seemed determined to continue, and I was riveted by her story.

I returned to the living room with a tray carrying the teapot, two fresh cups, and two more slices of cake. I poured the tea and offered a cup to Grandma along with a slice of cake, which she accepted. We finished our tea and cake, and she looked refreshed and composed and keen to continue her moving story.

"My George was such a quiet, kind, and peaceful man, I just could not imagine him fighting. He would do anything he could to avoid a fight, and here he was, going off to war. It just seemed incredible and unfair. We had a life to lead and dreams for the future, and now the prime minister was telling me that the man I loved was being taken from me to go and fight a war that had nothing to do with me or George. It was awful, truly awful.

"At the time, though, there was a strong sense of patriotism and that going to fight was doing the right thing for the country. I suppose we would call it propaganda now, but lots of messages on billboards and in newspapers were telling young people how brave they were to go to war and that they would be heroes. Although your grandfather was scared, he got caught up in this nonsense about being a hero and doing the right thing for Britain. I went along with this as I didn't want to dent his spirits before he left me." Tears streamed down her cheeks again as she said, "I didn't know if I would ever see him again, and I wanted us to part on good terms."

There was a long pause before she continued.

"We got married three weeks before he left for the war. He was to join the Gordon Highlanders and spend the first nine weeks doing his military training before being deployed. You must remember that there were no mobile phones in those days and no twenty-four-hour news channels. What was reported about the frontline was controlled completely by the British government. The day came, and off he went to join the war. Little did I know then that the only thing I would hear of him for the next five years would be a letter, smuggled out by the Red Cross, I received from him in 1942, saying he was still alive and that he thought of me every day. Then, in 1945, at the end of the war, I didn't know if he was dead or alive until I heard a knock at the door and there he stood in his army uniform. If memory serves me right, I fainted when I saw him.

"He told me about his time in the war over the first few weeks after he returned. It was like he needed to get his story out. Once it was out, though, he rarely spoke about it ever again. I never pushed him to speak about it, but I let him know that he could talk to me anytime. Occasionally the odd story would come out at an unexpected time, and I would just listen.

"George told me something of the fight at St. Valery. Fourteen thousand Gordon Highlanders were ordered to defend the town to let other British troops retreat to Dunkirk from the advancing German army. The plan was that the Gordon Highlanders would fall back and return to Britain before the Germans arrived, but the Germans arrived far quicker than had been anticipated, and a bloody battle began. Fighting raged for several days until the Gordon Highlanders were overrun and had to surrender. Of the fourteen thousand troops, only ten thousand still stood at the end of the battle. He told me that all the troops were rounded up and taken down to the beach. He was then taken to Poland as a prisoner of war, to a camp, I think it was called a stalag, near the city of Lodz, where he was forced to build roads for the next five years.

"This is where he encountered dogs. As he was marched to Poland, he had to walk a lot of the way, and was only put into trucks or buses for parts of the journey. As the soldiers marched, he told me that they were constantly marshalled by guards, who all had Alsatian dogs. These dogs would bark at them, and if someone got tired and started to lag, the dogs would bite their legs. George said there was no respite from these dogs, and they were always watching and looking for weakness.

"Once he arrived in Poland and was put to work building roads, they were set to work early in the morning. They would rise about 5 a.m. and be given a meager breakfast, often just a slice of bread and water. Then they were bussed out to the road they were working on. Work began at 6 a.m., and they worked until about 6 or 7 p.m. before they were bussed back again to camp. George said that guards stood by all day, watching them as they worked, and most of them had these fierce Alsatian dogs. As soon as someone paused or stopped for a break, the guard would approach with his dog, and it would snap and bite the prisoner. He said all the prisoners hated these dogs."

Grandma finished her story, and we both sat in silence. Her eyes were red from crying, and I felt a tear in my eye too. We let the pause continue comfortably for a while, sipping our tea and composing ourselves. Eventually she broke the silence.

"Hamish, that's all I can tell you about your grandpa just now, but I'm fascinated by your question and this connection to dogs you think has been passed down to you. You said that you thought it had left you now?"

"Yes," I replied.

"Good. Well, I hope it's helped my George in some way too," she said.

I thought of this conversation as I sat at the top of the monastery grounds, but I grew cold and headed back down to the monastery. Many of my fellow retreatants had now arrived. I recognized a few of them from previous retreats, and it was nice to chat with them briefly as we passed each other. The monks had made clear it was to be a silent retreat, so there was only so much we could say to each other. But a warm smile and holding our hands up to each other in gassho said all that needed to be said between fellow followers of "the way."

We all assembled for the evening's medicine meal, which is traditionally a soup. There were about thirty laypeople like me on the retreat, and we sat at three tables of ten. A monk sat at the head of the middle table. On this retreat, meals would be served and eaten formally. In Zen monasteries, this means that you eat in silence, a mealtime scripture is recited before you begin to eat, food is served to everyone in silence, and no one eats until everyone has their food; the monk signals when to start with a bow. There is something graceful and thoughtful about the process that I always enjoy.

Everyone on the retreat has their own plate and cutlery set waiting for them when they arrive. It always impresses me just how organized the monks are and the care and attention they put into everything. Your cutlery set is covered by a small drying cloth, and the whole set is covered by a large, white, square napkin. You identify your set by the small, rectangular piece of paper with your name on it. There is a rota pinned up on the notice board where people are expected to volunteer to serve the meals each day. I always put my name down to do this at least once during the week. It's nice to be involved and play your part in making the retreat work.

The formal meal ceremony has a seamless quality to it that makes me think about my relationship to food and greed. You're encouraged to take what you need, and you are expected to finish everything on your plate so that there's no waste. In Zen Buddhism we believe that everything has its worth. Whether it be a stick of celery or a humble carrot, we should eat it all and not discard it flippantly. When we eat, we are encouraged not to stare at other people or look to see how much food they have taken or judge how they're eating. As I sat there on the first night of segaki, the monastery's silence and sincerity hit me with the force of a sledgehammer, cracking me open like a nut. I felt such relief in stepping off the CEO hamster wheel for a week or so.

I thought about how I eat at home. I try to be mindful, but the monastery held up a mirror to me, and I saw my belly hanging slightly over the top of my trousers. It felt like the monastery was saying—in a respectful, nonjudgmental way—"You have maybe strayed from the path slightly, Hamish." In Buddhism, we try to avoid being judgmental and self-critical, and the Buddha taught to always follow the middle road—a path between self-denial and asceticism on one side and on the other a life of greed and overindulgence. In this moment I was aware that I'd fallen into comfort eating, partly due to stress. I tried to not judge myself but rather just be aware of this. Compassion is the key, and this includes compassion for yourself. I had only been in the monastery a few hours, and already I felt different—its teaching had begun.

After our medicine meal, I helped clean and dry the dishes in the kitchen, an experience I always enjoy. On a retreat, the monastery is catering for about sixty-five people, so the kitchen is on an industrial scale. The after-meal cleanup operation takes about forty-five minutes to an hour and usually involves about ten laypeople and six monks. You enter the kitchen, put on an apron, then wash your hands. A monk then gives you a task, and you do your best to complete it wholeheartedly. Silence is observed where possible. It is fascinating to watch people bob around the kitchen, mindfully working in harmony. The space is often tight, but people work together and get the task done.

There are two periods of thirty-five-minute meditation in the evening, broken up by ten minutes of walking meditation. After kitchen cleanup, I took a shower and headed for the first meditation of the retreat at 7:30 p.m. At the end of the meditation, we recited a scripture, "The Litany of the Great Compassionate One," before finishing at about 9 p.m. Then there was an hour of free time before lights-out at 10.

As expected, my mind was busy during these meditations. Thoughts came and went, gravitating towards work and what was happening at RCC. My mind would get caught up in memories of what was said at a board meeting, a leadership team meeting, or by a colleague. Every time I caught myself thinking about work, which was frequently, I gently brought my mind back to just sitting. My mind then wandered to the monastery, to my gratitude for being here, soaking in the atmosphere, its peace, its compassion, and its teaching. I once again brought myself back to my sitting.

The bell rang to signal the end of meditation, and we recited the litany, still sitting in meditation. Knees protesting, I rose with the others, and we bowed to one another. I left the Zendo and reveled in the atmosphere as I headed towards my room. I was tired. After brushing my teeth, I headed straight to bed.

The next day set out the routine we would follow for the rest of the week. The schedule below was posted on the notice board.

Schedule Monday – Friday

5:45   Wake Up

6.15   Meditation 2 x 35 minutes
(10 minutes walking)

7:40   Full morning service

8:10   Temple cleanup

8:50   Breakfast

9:20   Working meditation

10.50 Meditation 2 x 35 minutes
(10 minutes walking) (including talk)

12:10 Free time

12:30 Lunch, then free time

2:30   Meditation 2 x 35 minutes (10 minutes walking)

4:00   Tea, discussion, and questions with
Reverend Master Joshin

5:00   Meditation x 1 and evening service

6:00   Medicine meal, then free time

7:30   Meditation 2 x 35 minutes (10 minutes walking)

8:50   Vespers

9:00   Free time

9:45   Lights out

The first full day began, and in the morning my mind was noisy with work concerns. I simply kept letting go of these persistent thoughts. I discovered my chores for the rest of the week: for temple cleanup I was tasked to sweep and then mop the cloister floor, and for working meditation I was part of a five-person team helping a monk dig a drainage ditch. I really enjoyed working outdoors and the simple act of being given a manual task by the monks without my having to think about it; it stripped me of any pretense of being a CEO. I spend so much of my time planning and thinking and analyzing that simply being told to mop the floor and dig the ditch felt liberating.

The daily schedule included a talk during the 10:50 meditation period. I always feel that I listen more intently to a talk during meditation. On our first day, a minute or so in, I heard the voice of Reverend Master Jishu, the abbot of the monastery. I felt privileged to hear her speak. She was in her sixties but looked younger. I found her teachings to be profound, and when I first met her in person, I was impressed by her humility, sincerity, warmth, and good humor. She was about five foot six, slim, and she had a warm smile, blue eyes, and the traditional shaved head of a monk. She walked with a slow, purposeful step.

Her timeless voice broke the silence of the Zendo, and I sat up straight, eager to hear her teaching. "Why have you come to segaki? What has drawn you to this place this week? At this time of year, we reflect upon our own and others' impermanence."

The Zendo was silent, and her voice hit me like thunder as she spoke slowly with pauses between each sentence. "How do you feel about your own death? How do you feel about your own impermanence? How do you feel about the death of family and friends? Difficult questions for us all. Dogen, in the 'Rules for Meditation,' warns us that life passes as quickly as a flash of lightning; in a moment, life is gone. He encourages us to live well and train hard. In his work the *Shobogenzo*, the main written account of his life and practice, he wrote a chapter called 'Uji,' which is often translated as 'being time.' Is he suggesting time is not linear? Deep questions that are not easily answered. This week, we will explore these issues together."

She continued, "I ask you to think about your own mortality. What does this mean for your life and how you live it now? Does living a life of practice liberate you and me from suffering? Did the Buddha and the great teachers that came after him show us how to live well and free of fear? Are we able to face our own immortality and impermanence in a dignified way that is accepting of the ebb and flow of our lives? Do we really ever die? Are our deceased ancestors, family, and friends really gone, or is Dogen suggesting in 'Uji' that they are maybe still here in one sense? These questions are hard to answer with only our intellectual minds, but we can also use our life of practice and meditation to inform our understanding of life and death. We will avoid simplistic questions of whether ghosts exists or not, and go deeper into this."

Her voice stopped, and the silence seemed to roar. This was quite an opening remark, and I sat bolt upright on my bench as I absorbed her words.

Later that day, we had our first session of tea and questions with the reverend master. We assembled in the monk's library, waiting for her to arrive. When she entered the room, we all stood, hands in gassho. She walked to a seat in front of us and bowed before she sat down, facing us.

Reverend Master had decided to leave these sessions open with no planned structure; she wanted people to be free to speak their minds. She asked us to reflect upon what she had said during morning meditation and to use this week to really think about our own immortality and impermanence and explore this part of our life and practice. Then she sat back with a cup of tea in hand and simply asked, "So, what's on your mind?"

There was a long silence. I'm always impressed at how comfortable monks are in these silences. At the monastery I have observed how important and beneficial they can be. Rarely do I encounter these in my daily life when conversing with people; out in the world, there is always a rush to fill that void. Silence, although it can feel awkward, allows a different quality of conversation to arise. As people reflect deeply, their profound feelings and thoughts come to the fore.

Eventually someone began to speak; though I have learned to appreciate silence, I was relieved it was broken. A man called Alex talked about the death of his partner the year before. He spoke eloquently and movingly about his love for her and how grateful he was to assist her final few weeks in this world. She had been diagnosed with an aggressive cancer and died six weeks after the diagnosis. After Alex spoke, other members of the groups told similar stories of loved ones who had died. Some people expressed gladness at having had a chance to be there at the end, whilst others reflected on death and the need to live fully when we have the chance. It was difficult listening at times. The stories were moving, and many of my sangha brothers and sisters were upset as they spoke.

As I listened, I kept feeling Fudge's presence and picturing him, like he was in the room. I wondered if I should offer up my story about my karmic connection to him. But I kept quiet, and before long, the hour was up. Reverend Master signaled the end of the tea and discussion. *Why did I keep quiet?* I wondered during the next period of meditation. I reasoned that my dog's story did not quite fit with the moving stories about the loss of friends and family. But a small voice, an internal intuition, told me that this story should be shared. I resolved to do so before I left the retreat.

Tuesday unfolded with the usual mixture of meditation, working meditation, a talk, and some free time. We were now two and a half days into the sesshin, and I felt my mind beginning to change. It was still busy, and there was a lot of chatter and thoughts about work, but the pace and volume of this chatter had slowed. There were longer periods where I was aware that my mind was quiet.

Sitting in meditation for so long is an amazing but difficult experience. Not many people in today's modern world will ever come close. It's just not something you really get an opportunity to do or that people even think of.

What I find amazing is what my mind is capable of. In daily life, living in the world with the pressure of work and family, we hear our minds chatter and always think about the future or past. Most people will conclude that this is reality, the way things are. Meditating daily over years and sitting through many a sesshin has taught me that there is something deeper, and our minds can be in very different places if given the right conditions.

The hard part was that after only two and a half days of sitting on a meditation bench, my body was sore. My knees were the worst, but I also had pain in my upper back and shoulders. I used to be able to sit on a bench for a whole sesshin, all seven days, but halfway through Tuesday, I put away my bench and mat and meditated on a chair. This is perfectly okay, and many of the monks sit on a chair to meditate. *This is impermanence in action*, I thought. *Now that I have reached my late forties, my body just cannot do what it used to.* Buddhism has taught me to accept these changes and live gracefully with them.

There was an unusual talk on Wednesday morning during the 10:30 meditation, given by a fellow layperson rather than a monk. We sat in meditation, and then the familiar voice of Susan, whom I had met at Throssel several times before, split the silence of the Zendo. Her strong Geordie accent filled the room with purposeful teaching. I sat up on my chair, enthralled.

Susan explained that she was going to talk about uji, mentioned by reverend master the first day. Dogen's writings can be difficult for me and, I think, for everyone reading them today, but I'm always drawn to his teaching. My intuitive sense is that he is pointing to something deeper in us all. I was impressed that Susan had chosen this as her subject matter.

What followed had me mesmerized. Susan really got to the heart of what Dogen wanted to convey to us through this teaching in *Shobogenzo*.

The monks have taught me to listen on two levels when a talk is given during a meditation period. One level is to understand through the mind and intellect. The second is to understand it through intuition and feeling. Some things we just know to be true and beneficial, whilst not always being able to easily explain what has happened in words.

Susan spoke for about twenty minutes and explored the concept of uji with a depth I had never heard or read before. This wonderful woman was clearly practicing deeply; she spoke with such enthusiasm, clarity, and commitment. Her main point was that uji means that time itself is being, and all being is time. Uji is all the changing and dynamic activities that exist in the flow of becoming. Time is not as simple as it might appear. The worldly perception is that time is linear and always marching forward—but is it? Susan explained that Dogen suggested this is only one way of experiencing time. Time is imposed upon us and in some regards has been socially constructed with the advent of modernity and industrialization. Hunter and gatherer societies would have had a different experience of time. Only with the advent of industry was time imposed upon people, due to the need to begin and finish work at a certain time, to make production a seamless process. Before industrialization, time might have revolved around the seasons, and perhaps their experience felt more circular than linear.

Susan provided an example that struck me like a lightning bolt. She made her living by running her own dog rescue center. At the center she typically took in dogs who were older and had sadly been mistreated, and she provided space, love, and care so that they could live out the last few years of their lives peacefully. Over time she had seen many dogs die and as a result had developed a close friendship with the local vet.

Susan explained that she was not an advocate of euthanasia and only asked the vet to put down a dog if it was in pain. Her preference was to let the dog die naturally whilst ensuring it was not in pain. A few months previously, she had a dog called Rex, who became sick. Susan worried that he was in too much pain, so she called her vet, Michael Sewel, and explained the situation. Knowing that the dog must be very sick, Michael visited Susan's home as soon as he could.

When he arrived, he asked if he could observe the dog out in the garden.

It was a warm summer day, and the dog was sitting on the grass, occasionally shifting position. Michael observed Rex for twenty minutes before he was sure what to recommend to Susan. He called her out from her house, and they sat together on a bench, gazing at Rex. "Susan, I am certain that Rex is experiencing pain and discomfort that can't be made better with medication or surgery. Therefore, I recommend we put Rex out of his misery."

Susan had seen a lot of dogs die, and she trusted Michael. In her heart she knew that she had given Rex a peaceful final three years of his life. Before meeting Susan, Rex had several owners, who all found him too difficult to handle and eventually had given up on him. Susan was made of sterner stuff, though, and never gave up on Rex, and he enjoyed his life with her.

Susan fetched a table from her shed and covered it with a thick, comfortable blanket, and together she and Michael gently lifted Rex onto it. Michael prepared the injection and administered it to Rex, and Susan explained to us what happened next.

"As Michael prepared to administer the injection and Rex lay quietly on his soft blanket, there was a peaceful silence. Rex seemed to know it was his time to go, and was at peace with this. He lay still as Michael shaved the hair off his front leg. Rex glanced at us both momentarily but remained calm. I held Rex in my hands as Michael administered the injection, and Rex made no noise or movement whatsoever and just gave himself to the moment. Within seconds, Rex's body went limp, and within a minute he was lifeless."

Susan went on, "As Michael and I stood there together, one on either side of the table, a very surreal feeling came over me. I was later to find out Michael experienced the same thing. It is difficult to put into words, but it felt like time stood still. I felt an unusually strong sense of being at peace. The world seemed brighter, and I was acutely aware of the sounds of nature. The birds were singing, and I could hear the bees buzzing between plants. Neither Michael nor I spoke, and it felt hard to distinguish between me, Michael, and Rex. I knew that in that moment we were connected and that we were almost the same being, just slightly different. How I felt in that moment is hard to describe, but it was beautiful, graceful, as if I were being looked after by a force that I knew but which was beyond my understanding.

"I could not tell if this feeling lasted for thirty seconds, thirty minutes, or thirty years," she continued. "It felt like all three of us were being time or time being. In that moment, time didn't feel linear. It felt bigger than that, as if it stretched in all directions and swirled around us, going in a circular motion and then forwards and then backwards. I knew then that I was walking with the Buddhas and ancestors of old and with those yet to come. For a short time I felt the oneness of the world, past, present, and future.

"The silence of the moment was broken by a very shocked-looking Michael. I ensured that Rex was safe on the table and wrapped the blanket over him and kissed his forehead. I held Michael by the hand and led him to a seat. He looked dazed and bewildered. I asked him if he wanted tea. He merely nodded in reply. I made us both tea and went back out to the garden and sat with him in the warm sun and stayed silent until Michael spoke. In a bewildered voice, Michael asked, 'What was that? I've never experienced anything like that.'"

Susan said that she remained quiet and let Michael express himself and explore what had just happened. He said, "I'm an avowed atheist and have been all my life, and I never thought for the life of me that I'd experience something like that. What just happened, Susan? What did you feel? Is poor Rex okay and covered up?"

"Michael, you are not imagining things, I felt it too," Susan told him. "As to what it was, I can't say exactly. I can tell you I believe it was a good thing, but beyond our intellectual understanding."

She told Michael she was a Zen Buddhist. "In Zen we are open to the possibility that time and space are maybe not all that we assume. There are Zen scriptures that say all beings are time or time being, and if we are still and peaceful, in the moment, we can realize our connection to all beings, all times, past, present and future. My gut reaction is that we experienced something like that. Rex, you, and I were for a short moment fully aware of our connection to each other and all things and were being time."

I sat meditating as Susan told her story, impressed by how she had explained her understanding of uji and related it to some of her life experiences. I instantly thought of Fudge and felt at that moment he was by my side and still strongly connected to me. I had a powerful intuition that I was supposed to help Fudge move on and be at peace.

On the final day of segaki, there was going to be a ceremony that allowed us to help the spirits of loved ones move on and find peace. I needed to include Fudge in this; this seemed to be a major reason why I was at the monastery. The bell rang and meditation finished. I bowed with gratitude and was thankful for Susan and for her sharing her practice with us all.

The day continued, and before long, it was 4 p.m. and time for tea and questions with Reverend Jishu. We all got our tea and sat in silence, and Reverend Jishu invited us to offer up what was on our minds, what we were experiencing, so we could learn from one another. I felt a strong urge to speak and share my story. I raised my hands in gassho and began to talk about Fudge. I explained that I hadn't wanted to share this story prior to today as people were telling such poignant stories about family and friends they had lost. Although I had grieved deeply for many of my human family and friends, the death that had caused me the most grief and pain was my dog Fudge, and this had surprised me.

I explained the conversation with my grandma and my feeling that a strong karmic inheritance relating to a dislike of dogs had been passed from my grandpa to my dad and then to me. I struggled to get the story out, and felt emotional when I told it, but I managed to say all I wanted to say. This seemed to open the floodgates, and a range of stories were told by others about their deep connections to and loss of beloved animals. I think there were almost as many tears that day as there had been at the previous discussions. It showed me that I was not alone. I felt lighter after telling my story, and the discussion was deeply therapeutic.

The day came to an end, and after evening meditation, I retreated to my room. I felt lighter in spirit and sore in body. I did some basic yoga moves, trying to stretch the pain out of my muscles. Afterwards I lit the candle on the small altar in my room and sat on my chair in the corner and contemplated what had happened that day. I had really been struck by the directness of Susan's teaching on uji, and I sensed Fudge's strong presence with me again in my room.

The next day was the fourth full day of the retreat. From the start, I could tell that my mind had deepened. I felt alert, and the meditations flew past. My body felt less sore, or perhaps I was less aware of pain as I sat meditating. The mind chatter about work had almost stopped. Some thoughts came and went, but my mind felt at ease, and these thoughts did not distract me. I felt strongly connected to the others in the room, and internally I felt joyful and peaceful.

As there were just over thirty of us on the retreat, there were two rows of meditators on either side of the Zendo. I was in the back row, which meant I looked over the backs of those meditating in the front row. Throughout my meditations that day, strange sensations I had never before experienced took me by surprise. It felt as if the three people in front of me and I were sitting on a magic carpet, something that had the power to propel us through time and space.

I had the sensation that I was falling off my seat and had to steel myself. I glanced side to side to make sure everything was okay.

What was that? I thought. *A dizzy spell?* I settled my mind and concentrated on my meditation. The same thing happened again. I saw speed tracers coming from the people in front of me and had the feeling that we were twisting through time, turning left and right as we traveled on. This was an incredible sensation, and it felt very real.

I experienced this for much of the day, and each meditation filled me with joy, and I was oblivious to pain in my body. What it was I cannot say, but on reflection I believe that Susan's talk had really penetrated something in me. After four days of meditating, my mind had stilled enough to really hear, and more importantly feel, what she had said about uji. I was experiencing time being, or I was being time.

What's really amazing is that there was nothing truly special about these moments. It was just me quietening my mind to such a level that I felt time differently, as it really is, and I briefly felt the interconnectedness of all things in the past, present, and future. The Zen view on these experiences is of course to just note them, enjoy them when they arise, but not cling to them or see them as a sign of progress.

The next day of the retreat illustrated perfectly to me why this is the Zen view. I felt the pain in my back as soon as I woke up and was acutely aware of these aches and pains throughout the day's meditations. Whatever had happened yesterday was not present today. Impermanence in action.

Friday, the last full day of the retreat, arrived; this was the day of the segaki ceremony, which I was intrigued to see. The monks had asked us to write the names of any deceased loved ones on a piece of thick card shaped a little like a tombstone. These pieces of paper were to be placed on the altar during the ceremony, and monks were going to read out the names.

As with many things at the monastery, I was not quite sure how it was going to work or what was going to happen. I had visited often enough to know to simply trust the monks and be guided by them. There were some scriptures to be sung during the ceremony, and we had practiced them the day before. We were also given instruction on how the ceremony would proceed. Basically, there would be two lines of us on either side of the room. We would sing our scriptures and then move in a certain direction, slowly circumambulating the room. Each person would eventually pass the altar, where they would stop and light incense and offer it to the altar.

The moment came for the ceremony to begin. I was excited and nervous at the same time. I felt Fudge there in the room, and the anticipation of the lay trainees and monks. It was cold as all the windows in the ceremony hall were open to allow the hungry ghosts to come to the altar, which was adorned with lovely food, cakes of every description, and fruit that surrounded the Buddha on the altar.

The room was silent, and then I heard a noise that shook me to the core of my being—a bellowing sound emanating from just outside the monastery buildings. It was deep and loud, and the sound waves rippled through my body. I later learned that it was a conch shell being blown by a monk. When this sound stopped, the same sound erupted somewhere high up on the monastery grounds. Then another conch was blown lower down on the monastery grounds, its sound reverberating through the valley. The blowing of conch shells continued for another several minutes, and their deep resonance created a mysterious and contemplative atmosphere in the monastery and beyond. If this sound did not attract the attention of the spirits and gakis, nothing would.

Then came another sound in the distance that at first I could not make out. It sounded like cymbals being rubbed together, followed by a drumbeat. Slowly and steadily the sound drew closer and closer to the ceremony hall. A procession of monks appeared at the door and slowly entered the room. At the front was Reverend Master Jishu, followed by Reverend Claire, who was slowly beating a drum, and behind her was Reverend Lamont, holding a pair of large cymbals. Behind these three monks was a procession of about twenty monks walking slowly with their hands held in gassho. The monks filed into rows in front of the lay practitioners, and Reverend Master Jishu stood in the middle, directly in front of the altar. At this point Reverend Claire and Reverend Lamont quickened their pace. The slow drumming grew faster and faster, as did Reverend Lamont's cymbals.

This was incredible to watch, and the atmosphere of the normally quiet and peaceful monastery became electric. The drums and cymbals were now being played so fast that my head was spinning, and the two monks playing them looked lost in a trance until they finally finished with a loud crash of the cymbals and last booming beat of the drum. Then silence. Reverend Master Jishu bowed, and as she did so, there was another blow of a conch just outside the door of the monastery.

Reverend Jishu spoke as she stood in front of the altar. "All beings are welcome here, and we welcome you now. Please find sustenance on our altar and be able to satisfy your desire for peace. Use this moment to hear the dharma and use it to help you find the truth of all existence and to find your true home." Whilst the Reverend Master offered incense to the altar, we sang one of the scriptures we had practiced the day before.

We started our circumambulation of the ceremony hall, slowly walking and singing the "Scripture of Avalokitesvara"; this scripture is full of stories of Avalokitesvara doing great deeds to help people who have cried out for her help. I heard whispering and noticed two monks standing on either side of the altar, reading the names of all the beings whose names we had placed on the altar. They read these names over and over again with urgency and conviction. I picked out Fudge's name twice, although I think his name was probably mentioned more than that.

The atmosphere felt incredible and surreal. The blowing of the conches, the drumming, cymbals, and now this deeply moving ceremony made me feel like time had stopped or I was living in a different time or age. I could not help but feel that something I had never experienced was happening in this room. I did not know what it was, but I knew intuitively that it was good. The room fell silent and the ceremony was over. The monks left in a slow and quiet procession. Reverend Hubert stayed behind, and we all bowed in unison with him to mark the finish of the ceremony.

In the free time following the ceremony and before lunch, I chose to take a stroll. I made my way up to the top of the monastery grounds and sat at the same spot I had sat on the first day. I felt very different now compared to then. My mind was quieter, and my physical body felt different. I did feel pain from so much meditating, but I could tell this was superficial and would soon go once I returned home to my normal routine, and despite the pain, my body felt more relaxed, and I felt no numbness or tightness in my muscles.

And I thought, *What is reality? What is more real—monastic life or everyday life, the world of work and striving for position, things, wealth, and comfort and the terrible ecological implications of the modern lifestyle? What would my board of directors or my senior colleagues think if they saw their Buddhist CEO sitting here? What will friends and family say when I return and tell them about my week here?*

Tears formed in my eyes and dripped down my cheeks. These were not tears of sadness but rather tears of contentment. In this moment, I felt that the monastery, the monks, my fellow lay trainees, and the opportunity to meditate so deeply over a prolonged period had shown me a glimpse of truth. I felt strongly that human life is more than the boardroom, more than success, more than trivial disagreements amongst staff, more than acquiring things, and more than the throwaway society and the ecological crisis it has unleashed. In this moment, I realized that there is something in us all that is peaceful and compassionate. All we need are the right conditions for this to manifest.

Contentment comes from living well and being deeply connected to the world, people, all beings, and the earth. I had found more peace and contentment living with the monks for a week than I would on any holiday to a far-flung part of the world or from owning a new car or the latest "must-have" gadget. I had not looked at my phone for a week and felt all the better for it, and my mind had benefitted from that break. Life is precious, people are precious, all beings are precious, and the earth is precious. I sat and let this sink in as I gazed out across the Pennine Hills, silent and contemplative, deeply moved by the week that had now almost passed. Oyster catchers called from the field above. They were the only witness to my tears.

What does this mean for me? Does this mean anything at all? I knew deep down that I wasn't fully happy in my CEO role anymore. Yes, I could do it well and had dragged a company up by the scruff of its neck and made it a success. I was proud that I'd achieved this and genuinely grateful for the opportunity RCC had given me. Being a CEO allowed me to grow as a person in so many ways, but I could no longer ignore how the role was affecting my health.

This week had shown me another life was possible. *But how can I incorporate the monastery's more peaceful and contemplative rhythms into my life?* Life is complicated, and it's not easy to give up a good salary once you and your wife and children have gotten used to the lifestyle it allows. Quite what that way ahead was to be, I couldn't say; I just knew I wanted to continue to practice this Buddhist life, with all the contentment and peace that it brings.

Saturday arrived, and the retreat was due to finish after breakfast. The first meditation period was at 7:15, an hour later than the rest of the week. The monks wanted us to have a gentle morning before we all headed off on our long journeys home. I sat in the final meditation period with mixed feelings. I looked forward to seeing Beth and the boys, but as always, leaving this incredible place gave me a sense of melancholy. I heard birds calling and the wind blowing as I sat in that quiet Zendo for the last time, soaking up the peacefulness. The meditation finished all too quickly with the ringing of two soft bells. I bowed deeply to the monks, to this place, Throssel Hole, and to my fellow lay trainees, feeling deep gratitude for them all.

CHAPTER 8

The Fellowship of the CEOs

> The way is perfect, subtle, hard to perceive.
>
> It's like drinking water.
>
> You know how hot or cold it is
>
> But cannot tell others.
>
> —*Bodhidharma*

As my experience of being a CEO changed from an exhilarating roller-coaster ride to the daily grind of battling against staff and board members' petty gripes, I wondered if I could find support. But where does a CEO go for support?

I attended a few events put on by organizations in Scotland that offer support to CEOs in the charity sector. Though the events were well delivered, and I enjoyed them and learned from them, I wanted something deeper. I wanted to get under the bonnet and into the psyche of my fellow CEOs. Was I alone in feeling disillusioned with the role? Did other CEOs struggle with staffing issues, their board, and had they faced the kinds of difficulties I had encountered on my leadership journey?

I could not turn to any of my staff, not even the senior ones. The CEO sets the vision for the company and leads by example. I felt a strong obligation to support my senior staff so they could go on and support their teams. For that reason, it wasn't appropriate for me to say, "Hey, guys, you know what, I'm struggling with things today." I was comfortable with open discussions with staff and being transparent if I didn't know immediately how to tackle a challenging issue, and I was comfortable looking for a team answer, but I always wanted to show that I was strong and positive and enjoying my work. How could others be motivated to do their best for RCC if they had doubts about their CEO's commitment and enthusiasm?

I also wanted to understand the relationship between other CEOs and their boards of directors. Working closely with a board of directors is an experience few people will ever have. The CEO is supposed to act as the link between the board and the rest of the company. A good CEO skillfully ensures they're kept abreast of what is happening in the company and that the board's strategic vision is carried out on a day-to-day basis. To achieve this balance is no easy task, and I have found working with the board fascinating on one hand and deeply frustrating on the other.

My board has challenged me, supported me through thick and thin when I needed them, and deeply frustrated me at times. I have no doubt that board members would feel similarly about me if they were asked.

RCC's constitution stated we could have up to twelve directors, and during my time as CEO, the number fluctuated from time to time but averaged about ten at any given time. Some of the directors on the board had been there for many years, some as long as a decade. In 2015 the board recognized that this probably was not healthy in the long term and that a certain amount of turnover would mean the board stayed fresh, with new ideas being brought to the table by new faces. They decided that directors could serve two periods of three years before renouncing their role.

At RCC, our directors came from a range of backgrounds. Most, but not all, were recently retired people who had previously held very senior posts throughout their careers. On retiring they genuinely wanted to use those skills to help grow and develop a charity that meant something to them. Many of them were motivated to make a difference in society, and this is something I admired about all of them.

On our board we had two ex–senior bankers, three previous directors of services of local authorities, a lawyer, HR consultant, two business owners, the CEO of another local charity, and another director who worked for a national charity. I respected them all, and on a one-to-one basis they were fantastic. Overall they backed me when the chips were down, including when I faced difficult staffing issues, and they recognized that these situations were not easy for me to deal with. I appreciated their support on these matters. But although my board members were good people with a wealth of knowledge, working with them challenged me as a CEO and as a Buddhist.

One of the first realizations I had when I first came into the role was the illusion of absolute authority. I suspect most people imagine that the CEO can do as they please, with little or no scrutiny. This might be the case if the CEO owns the company outright, but not if they report to a board of directors. The board took a very keen interest in every aspect of the company and expected regular reports on performance, finances, human resources, health and safety, and more. If just one person on the board asked an unexpected question, the whole board meeting could take a strange twist. This was not just pertinent to my board but was a common occurrence across all companies, I was to find.

Once, when I had been in post around two years, we were reviewing the financial year that had just passed, and I also asked the board to review and approve the budget set for the new financial year. I had gained enough experience with the board to know that I should be prepared for anything to happen at our meetings. Despite this, I went into it with a feeling that all would be positive. I was reporting a surplus of about £50,000, which had improved from the previous year's surplus of £20,000. In the years immediately prior to me becoming CEO, the company had made significant six-figure losses.

As well as performing well financially, our services delivered to roughly 800 more customers annually than we had previously, due to changes I had made to how we managed services. Our customer satisfaction was higher than RCC had ever achieved. I thought before the meeting, *What can go wrong? The board will be delighted when they see the finances.*

When the chairman asked me to talk through the financial report I'd provided to all the board members, I was brief and stuck to the headline points. We had made a surplus for the second year running, and the main reasons for the improved financial position were streamlining our overhead costs, particularly by reducing the number of external contractors we used; maximizing the income we were entitled to draw down from national and local government contracts, something we had not done previously; and attracting funding for two new services that would contribute to a greater projected income. In addition, we had raised £650,000 through fundraising efforts.

In Zen Buddhism you are meant to live in the moment, not expecting anything to fall into your lap and not looking for praise or thanks but rather living your own life, free of these expectations. Despite trying to practice this in my life, I did expect something from my board that night. I expected just a little nod to say, "Well done, Hamish. We recognize you have turned this company around."

After my update, Norman asked me to move on to the budget forecast for the financial year we had just entered. Our budget was always set in April, even though the financial year had just started. We did this because so much of our funding from national and local government was not finalized until this time, which made setting the budget any earlier pointless. I put forward a budget forecast of increasing our surplus for a third year to £91,000. I explained that the slight improvement in forecast was primarily down to the new projects that we had secured funding for. The board fell silent again, and Norman asked if there were any questions.

Jim, a long-standing board member, asked why the legal fees budget had been forecast to increase by £20,000. I explained this was because analysis of previous years had shown that we had overspent on this budget line by between £15,000 and £23,000 for each of the last three years and I was keen to make the forecast as accurate as possible. Jim continued, "Why have we overspent on this budget line previously?" I explained that each year we had experienced unexpected legal costs related to staffing issues.

I thought this would end the conversation, but to my surprise, Jim said, "I don't like this. What type of organization have we become? Who puts aside money to pay for tribunals or being sued?"

Not only did the comment hurt, but the way in which it was said stung. Jim had a look of disgust on his face, and he could not look at me as he said it. He was looking at other board members with an incredulous expression as he shook his head. Another board member, Mark, agreed that he felt very uncomfortable about this and that we should not be budgeting for these possible eventualities and should just deal with them if they arose. This sparked a debate, with everyone chipping in their own negative view on this being included in the budget. I sat back and just watched and listened.

The debate was surreal. For fifteen minutes it felt like they didn't even notice I was still in the room. Heads were shaken; disappointment was expressed. What did this say about the company? Were we becoming too draconian and losing our moral compass?

Anger rose in me, and my chest tightened. My pride was hurt, and I felt a deep sense of disbelief, but I steadied my breath and focused on calming my emotions. My inner voice suggested this was a great opportunity to practice the Buddhist way and let go of my ego and feelings of being let down. As they ran out of steam after several minutes, they seemed to notice that I had gone quiet.

Norman, who was chairing the meeting, asked, "Hamish, there has been a robust conversation about this budget line. What is your view on this?"

I paused in what felt like an awkward silence and then decided to give them my honest opinion. "To be honest, I'm a little surprised and disappointed in the conversation. We have not become too draconian nor lost our moral compass, as evidenced by our continual appearance as a company listed in the *Sunday Times* Top 100 companies to work for in the UK and other prestigious awards that have all been awarded in recognition of how we treat our employees. Other staff surveys and awards consistently show our staff feel valued, supported, and treated compassionately. The board have asked for an accurate and realistic budget after several years, before my time, where they were wildly optimistic. I have simply included this extra line in the budget because the reality is that we have had to deal with these costs for the last three years, and I simply thought it prudent to budget for something like this happening.

"This doesn't mean in any way that I expect it to happen," I continued, "and I certainly don't want it to happen. I would remind board members that the information I am presenting to you this evening is positive. After several years of losses, we have made a surplus two years running, and this shows a healthy improvement in RCC's fortunes. Not only that, but I'm forecasting an even healthier position this financial year. This is a draft budget, and as board members you've every right to ask me to remove this line from the budget if it displeases you. However, please do not let one line in the budget overshadow what should be a positive meeting, and recognize the positive changes that have been and are still being made."

This seemed to bring them back to reality a bit. Norman could see I was annoyed, and he did his best to bring some composure back to the conversation. "Points well made, Hamish, and yes, I should remind board members that the financial position of the preceding year and the forecast for the year ahead is a very positive position. I thank Hamish and his team for delivering this vastly improved position. I do think it's appropriate that the board does consider the moral implications of how and why we set the budget as we do. We are an organization that strives to be ethical, and we want to ensure we maintain this stance. Can I therefore suggest that we include this in the budget, but it will be termed as a contingency budget for unforeseen events." People round the table nodded, and although I was thankful to Norman for this suggestion, it didn't really change things.

The rest of the meeting went on in a similar flat and uninspiring fashion. I sat through it feigning interest, and soon it was over. I went home deflated and frustrated. This board had presided over a farce before I'd arrived. I'd pulled the company out of the abyss and turned it into a high-functioning organization that was now financially viable. But they were sitting around arguing about a minor line in the budget. It felt wrong.

These thoughts and frustrations tumbled through my mind in meditation for several days and weeks afterwards. I could not help that these types of conversation dented my morale. Beth had come to expect a defeated look on my face after board meetings. It was hard enough being the CEO. Although I respected my board members, I felt they could deal with conversations like this more skillfully. Was it my ego? Had all these years of Buddhist practice been in vain?

By chance, I'd spoken to two fellow CEOs at a conference who, over a coffee, expressed how alone they too felt in their roles and that there was nobody to off-load to, no allies in sight. They felt it wasn't appropriate to off-load their concerns and frustrations with their chairman, board members, or senior staff.

This made me feel better, validating my feelings that I wasn't alone or unique after all. I suggested that we try to establish a forum for CEOs where we could meet in confidence and offer support to each other. They were delighted, and we arranged to meet a few weeks following.

The three of us met, and it became clear that we all faced challenges. Our roles were highly complex, sometimes with no clear answers. We agreed to establish a peer support group and drew up a list of CEOs who we knew personally and thought would be interested in becoming involved. Everyone we invited responded positively, keen to get involved.

We all met for the first time a few weeks later. There were ten of us in total, and at the first meeting we set out the remit of the group. We agreed that we must treat everything said in the meeting in confidence and that we should try to attend as regularly as possible. The group was to be a forum for raising our challenges in a safe and supportive environment. When any of us raised a challenge we were experiencing, the others would be there to offer ideas on how to confront the difficulty and challenge our own thinking on the problem. We would take turns hosting the meetings at our respective organizations, and whoever was hosting that day would chair the meeting. I felt quite excited after the first meeting; there had clearly been enthusiasm in the room. Finally, I was going to get under the bonnet of other CEOs.

The next meeting came around quickly and was held in the boardroom at Sports Hub, a local charity that worked in disadvantaged communities, engaging the community in various initiatives to get fit and healthy. Their CEO, Gregor Williams, chaired the meeting, and after welcoming everyone, we helped ourselves to coffee and tea. He asked if anyone had any issues they wanted to raise. Desperate and bursting to raise mine, I jumped in first.

"Guys, it's so nice to be here today. I've been keen for this meeting to happen for a while now, as I've often wondered if I'm alone in some of the challenges I face. I have one particular challenge that I would like to raise with you, and it relates to my board and chairman and how I interact with them."

As I said this, a few of my fellow CEOs wore knowing smiles. I went on to explain how I feel deflated after board meetings; I explained the recent tensions between my chairman and me. I gave balance to what I said and made clear that I respected my board members and my chairman, and I recognized the wealth of experience and knowledge they brought, and also that they'd supported me during difficult times, but despite that, I still found them challenging to deal with collectively.

A discussion began. Every CEO in the room said that their biggest challenge was their board. There was unanimous agreement that most people's boards were made up of highly skilled people who were well intentioned. However, as a group they all struggled with their boards, and one of the great skills a CEO needed was knowing how to manage their board. The relationship between CEO and chairperson was also viewed as a vitally important but tricky one that could easily go wrong. They felt that the recent tensions between my chairman and me were unfortunate, but all agreed that these types of situations arise periodically, and they had experienced similar situations.

A couple of my fellow CEOs wanted to tell their stories as well, and I was eager to hear. Joan, CEO of a housing charity, told us all an incredible story that happened years previously when she was working for a large charity in London. "About fifteen years ago, I went on holiday for three weeks to Australia to visit my son and newborn grandson. I thought all was well with my organization and my relationship with the board. I'd been in post for about eight years at this point, and I'd helped build a strong organization, and the services we delivered to the homeless community were effective and financially robust. It was well respected in the community, too. I'd no reason to think anything was wrong. So off I went on my trip, and I had the time of my life spending time with my family, and came back to London feeling refreshed, relaxed. This feeling didn't last long," she laughed.

"On the Sunday evening before I was due to go back to work," she continued, "I got a phone call from Sheila, one of my board members. She rarely phoned me at home, so I knew straightaway that something was up; I could hear it in her voice. I almost fell over when I heard what she had to say. In my absence, the board had decided to terminate my employment! To say I was shocked would be an understatement. A board member who I'd never had many dealings with before and had only joined the board about four months earlier had started a campaign against me in my absence. She had gone around to all the board members, telling them things that were apparently going wrong with the company and how it was all my doing. Enough board members were persuaded by the arguments, and an emergency meeting was called in my absence. The decision was made to terminate my employment. Thankfully three of my board members stood up for me, including Sheila, but the other eight were persuaded by this campaign."

"What did you do and what happened in the end?" I asked.

"I was grateful to Sheila for telling me so at least I was going into work aware of what was waiting for me. I went in early and prepared for how I was going to tackle this. I'm a member of a trade union, so I contacted them immediately, and luckily, they had an office close by in central London and offered to see me right away. They were brilliant, and as I suspected, they saw many legal, moral, and ethical problems with my board's stance. They advised me to call their bluff, which I did. I went back to the office and wrote an email to all my board members, copying my trade union into the email.

"I told them that I was aware of their plan to dismiss me and that I was horrified and deeply disappointed by their actions, which fell well below the standards they were supposed to be setting. I told them I had no intention of leaving my post and that I had explained the situation to my union, who were supporting me with this situation, and I requested a meeting with the full board and my union to get to the bottom of the situation.

"I also made clear that I was willing to take legal action against the board. Cutting a long story short, we had that meeting, and the whole thing fell apart. The three board members who had supported me all along stood up and said they were disgusted at the other board members' actions and this was no way to behave towards anyone, let alone the CEO, who they felt had done a very good job over the years and had their full backing. From there, the chairman resigned, as did four others, and the whole thing was dropped and seen for the farse and political maneuvering it was. But it shows you how vulnerable we are as CEOs to the potential whim of a board member. I had loved that job, but I never really got over that incident, and ultimately it led me to leave and move back up to Aberdeen."

Others began to open up. Jacklyn, CEO of a large recycling charity, told a story that was common amongst the group, where a chairman or board member had spoken to them in a way that was totally unacceptable. Jacklyn's chairman, Andrew Winterburn, was CEO of a large and well-known hotel chain that did business across Europe. She explained that she respects her chairman and has built a strong and supportive relationship with him over the last few years. However, she had to work hard at building this relationship, and it took a while to establish proper professional boundaries. Many chairpersons want to make a difference in society and use their skills, usually after a long and distinguished career, to help improve and grow a charity. When Andrew became her chairman, the organization was going through a difficult time. They had lost a couple of big contracts and had just lost a senior member of staff in circumstances that were not ideal.

Recently, they had made unsuccessful bids for new contracts. Andrew had only been in the role five months at the time, and he wanted to make his mark and really wanted to win these contracts. Jacklyn told us that one day he unexpectedly burst into her office and started to shout and say things like, "This is fucking unacceptable that we have not won these contracts. What the fuck is going on in this place, and what the fuck are you doing about it, Jacklyn?"

As Jacklyn told this story, there were a few smiles and nods round the table. "I was shocked, really shocked," she said. "I took a deep breath and composed myself, and then I spoke calmly to Andrew. 'Andrew, that might be the way you're used to speaking to people in your hotels, but it is highly inappropriate for you to talk to me like that. I insist that you never address me like that again. I am happy to discuss any matter with you, and like you I am also disappointed that we didn't win these new pieces of work. However, I am more concerned about learning from the feedback from our bid to ensure we win the next bid we submit.'"

Jacklyn explained that her chairman calmed down and apologized.

He said he was just having a bad day and he boiled over. They sat together in her office after this incident and spoke for two hours. They cleared the air and agreed on how to communicate going forward, and their relationship has been professional ever since.

I came to love these CEO meetings and grew to know most of the CEOs very well. We met every eight weeks or so as a group, and I started to meet up with some of them on a one-to-one basis for coffee because it was challenging getting everyone together sometimes. I came to think of this group as the fellowship of the CEOs.

What struck me was that every single one of us was almost constantly dealing with a situation or multiple situations that could be classed as highly stressful, and I think this is particularly true of charity CEOs. Charity CEOs lead organizations on extremely tight budgets, and because they don't have lots of money, often they have no finance directors, HR directors, nor legal departments, and staff, including the CEO, end up performing several roles themselves. Few people on the planet will ever experience what that feels like.

One day, I met an old acquaintance for coffee to discuss some business ideas. Brian Lawton was a successful businessman in Aberdeen, and he had been a director of a successful oil company. What I admired about Brian was his social ethos. Despite working in the private sector, he had founded a successful charity in the city that encouraged children and young people to get involved with sports.

I met Brian for a coffee in Kirriemuir, a small town a few miles from where he lived in the county of Angus. We got to speaking about the role of a CEO in the charity sector, and I was struck by what he said. It was his view that what we are asked to do in our roles compared with what he had experienced at the senior level in the oil industry was night and day; the workload and what the charity sector CEO had to deal with was far more arduous than anything he had seen in the private sector.

I asked him why he thought this. Brian said that the oil industry was generally so well resourced that someone always dealt with HR or finance on his behalf; he didn't have to get heavily involved. In contrast, he knew quite a few of the leading charity CEOs in Aberdeen, and he could see they were under immense pressure and dealing with more complex challenges. It was refreshing to hear this view, and it lent further weight to my growing feeling that the stress and difficulty of the role was seldom understood in wider leadership circles.

This made me wonder again about my own health, and how this role was affecting it. Were all these strange symptoms that had appeared over the last seven years a sign of stress?

The fellowship of the CEOs became very important to me. Meeting people in the same role and talking candidly about our challenges was liberating for us all. Finally, we had found fellowship and support that could help us to in some way cope with the stresses and strains of our daily jobs.

Through the fellowship, I became close friends with a guy called Malcolm, the CEO of a charity that supported people with multiple sclerosis (MS). Malcom had become the CEO nine years ago and really enjoyed building the charity up; it was now recognized as an excellent organization, offering a fantastic range of different support services to people suffering from MS and their families. But he had hit upon some difficult times recently.

I would meet Malcolm for coffee in the Washington Café down at Aberdeen Beach. This brought back memories of visiting there regularly with Beth in our carefree days before family and leadership came along.

During meetings with Martin, we met early in the morning for breakfast and chewed over some of the leadership issues we were both facing. I enjoyed hearing Malcom's take on things, and I think he enjoyed hearing mine. Though typically we met up every couple of months, it dawned on me one day that it must have been about four months since I'd last seen him. Later that very week, he sent me an email asking to meet up for breakfast at the usual place. We agreed to meet the following Friday.

I arrived at the Washington just after 8:30, and Malcom was already sitting at our favorite seat at the window, a quiet table slightly apart from the main body of the restaurant and boasting beautiful views out to sea. We shook hands, both pleased to see each other. We made small talk, I ordered my usual veggie breakfast, and Malcolm ordered a bacon roll. As soon as the waiter took our order, Malcom asked if I'd heard he'd been unwell.

"No," I answered, "but it did occur to me that I hadn't seen or heard from you in a while."

"So, let me tell you my story, my friend. At our CEO meeting, I think I told you all that I had encountered some problems with senior staff. These issues were mainly with my finance manager, who had become difficult and obstructive. I felt that he was withholding information from me, and at times I suspected he deliberately wanted me to look foolish in front of my board."

"In what way?" I asked.

"He was supposed to provide monthly management accounts within five days after the month end. We'd agreed to this timescale, and we were to sit down and review the management accounts together before reporting the figures to the board. Now, you would think that if you were the finance manager and you had agreed to this with your CEO, you might just see this as an important deadline. Well, the end of every month would come and go, but these figures never appeared.

"This drove me crazy," he went on, "but I kept my cool and would calmly walk down to his office and ask if he had the management accounts. There was always some excuse: 'I do not have the figures yet,' or 'I am just doing the final calculations.' He would agree to get them to me the following day, but even then, he often would not appear at my office, and I had to go looking for him again. By this time, my chairman would be asking to discuss the accounts with me, and I would have to make an excuse as to why they were not ready, which made me look and feel stupid.

"Eventually I sat him down and asked if everything was okay.

'What do you mean?' was his response. I said, 'I'm growing frustrated that the management accounts are not ready on the agreed timescale. Every month I have to come to your office and ask where they are, and I feel that when I ask you for the accounts, you become defensive and difficult. I then end up having to explain to the chairman why they're late, and I feel foolish. If the deadline we have set for the accounts is too early, then I'm happy to review this. I would also ask that in the future you come to me if they are going to be late and explain why, rather than me having to come and seek you out.'"

"Seems a fair approach to me, Malcolm," I said.

"Interesting you say that, Hamish, as I thought so too, but he flew off the handle and said that he didn't like the way I was speaking to him, that he felt I was threatening and he felt intimidated. I couldn't believe it, but I took a deep breath and calmly explained to him that I'm the CEO and I want to support him, but I have every right to expect deadlines to be met, especially when the finance function is so important.

"Cutting a long story short," he continued, "he agreed to produce the management accounts by the fifth working day after the month end. He clarified that he didn't think this was too much to ask and agreed that it was his responsibility to notify me if there was to be any holdup in the future. What happens at the end of the following month? No management accounts, and he doesn't come to see me to explain why, and I had to go looking for him to raise the issue again. When I spoke to him, he was indifferent and resistant, and I just couldn't contain myself and I lost my temper.

"I called him out and asked what the hell was going on—just what kind of game was he playing? Of course, he left the room in tears and submitted a formal complaint against me. Our chairman and another board member had to interview me as part of an investigation. I'd been under a lot of stress just keeping the company going, and now I had this on my plate. Not only that, but it transpired that he had spoken to his senior colleagues in our leadership team, and they had clearly been influenced by him and became frosty towards me. Something just went snap in my head. That is the only way I can explain it. It just went snap. The job is hard enough as it is, and I had always tried to support and develop my leadership team, and I felt I didn't deserve this."

"What do you mean, Malcolm, when you say your mind went snap?" I asked.

"It's not easy to explain, but I felt like something shifted in my mind. I felt numb and indecisive, and reality just seemed different to me. I could tell I was out of step with the world and not myself. My wife and kids could tell I was different, and they were concerned for me and pleaded with me to go to the doctor. After I told the doctor my symptoms, he said something interesting. He said, 'What is it about all you CEOs?' 'What do you mean?' I asked. 'I've CEOs in here frequently with similar symptoms, usually resulting from severe stress, and it makes me wonder about that role, especially charities.' The doctor signed me off for the next three months, and I just came back to work early last week. I feel great now, but I'm right back into a really stressful situation again, and to be honest I'm looking for another job before this one makes me ill again."

I was fascinated by what Malcom's doctor had said about so many CEOs coming to see him with stress. This was an insight into a hidden world. *Is it worth it?* I wondered.

I looked in the mirror one morning and didn't like what I saw. I looked tired, my face was redder than it should be, and I was carrying more weight than ever before, particularly around my waist. I had become two stone heavier since taking on the role; before this, there was hardly a pick of fat on me. I was forty-nine but felt much older.

In the eyes of the world, I suppose it looked like I was successful and achieving what many people aspire to. I got immense satisfaction from knowing that I was providing for my family and able to give them things I couldn't have dreamed of before becoming a CEO. I'd provided the boys fantastic opportunities, and they really enjoyed traveling, going to concerts and the theatre, and Beth and I could pay for any sports they wanted to try. We could pay for driving lessons and their first cars. Even though Beth and I were happy even when we didn't have much money the first twenty years together as a couple (and she never asked for anything), it did feel good being able to pay for her to do special things with her friends and family for a change.

But somewhere deep in my soul, I felt emotionally and spiritually flat, overweight, and unhealthy. My meditation practice seemed stale, and sometimes I felt like I was going through the motions, playing at being a Buddhist. Something was happening to my body and my mind, but I couldn't quite say what it was just yet.

CHAPTER 9

My Tingling Hands

BALLOCHBUIE

I remember the Lawrence Tree

toppling towards the infinite

unbowed by the stars

tentacle branches probing

a dense black hole of foliage

harvesting colossal power.

Here in the Ballochbuie

where great pines still flourish

another of equal majesty has

propelled itself out from the heather

and blueberry where I lie

towards the vaulting depths of heaven

an eruption of armoured plate

and scale through granite rock

a tectonic fusion of wood and stone

locked and anchored

like some beam

holding this place together

a beanstalk tempting me

to leave earth

climb by column and tower

into the undying light

the implacable burning

of a million green fuses

stoking their power

in the depths of the wood

—*Brian Lawrie*

It was late November 2019, and I sat in my office, writing the papers for an upcoming board meeting. Earlier that morning, I'd sat in meditation and kept getting a feeling that something wasn't right with me.

My fingers had become sore at the tips again, but it felt different this time. Not only were they sore at the fingertips, but I had a numb and tingling sensation in my hands. I developed the same feeling in my feet. It was subtle, but I'd never felt this before. What worried me more was that I began to feel dizzy, something I'd never experienced before either. I had felt this way for a couple of weeks now and initially hoped it might disappear of its own accord. Perhaps it was just a virus working its way through my system.

But two weeks after I first noticed these sensations, it became clear that they were not just going to disappear. I phoned my doctor and got the earliest appointment, two weeks hence. In the meantime, I continued to work away as normal, but the sensations got worse each day. My concentration was deteriorating too. It was subtle at first, but in a meeting with several people, I found it difficult to comprehend everything that was being said. My mind felt foggy. Information came into my brain, but I wasn't processing it in the right way.

Though I was slightly anxious about my colleagues, I think these changes went unnoticed. I continued to rise early each morning to meditate, but it became a chore; for the first time I felt I really had to push myself to enter the Zendo every day. Although slightly troubled by these new feelings and sensations, I approached them as I did the rest of my life—with a Buddhist approach. I tried to not get attached to any view I had about what might be wrong with me. I just let thoughts of fear or anxiety come and go from my mind. Overall, I continued to feel grounded and peaceful, but I knew something was different.

My appointment with the doctor came. My hands and feet continued to tingle and feel numb, and other symptoms had manifested: a sore shoulder that made it difficult to move my arm backwards and really hurt when I pulled on a jacket; a sunburnt feeling on the skin outside of my left shoulder, with no accompanying redness nor swelling, and I hadn't been in the sun; a patch on the left of my abdomen, about the size of my fist, felt completely numb; my face also felt numb at times, and the dizziness worsened. I had become quite worried about this situation.

When I arrived at the health center, I explained my symptoms to Dr. Simpson, and she listened intently. "Wow, you really have a lot going on," she said. She took the view that there was a range of things that could be causing these symptoms, and the first step was to run some tests. She asked if I'd have some time off over the festive period.

"Yes, two weeks," I said.

Dr. Simpson said she wanted me to take it easy at work until the festive holidays and really try to relax during my time off and referred me to the practice nurse to have blood tests taken. She was going to test my thyroid and test me for diabetes, arthritis, and for any vitamin and mineral deficiencies. I agreed to relax as much as possible over the festive period, and I'd take things as easy as I could at work until then. I made an appointment to see her on 9 January. Dr. Simpson wanted to see how I was after a holiday, and she'd discuss my test results with me in the new year. If anything more serious showed up, she'd call me sooner.

I had been well all my life until this point. You do not know how you'll deal with something like this until it happens to you. I felt calm in one sense, but my mind constantly wandered to what could be wrong with me. My doctor was testing for all sorts of things, and I found myself looking up the symptoms of these conditions. It seemed like any of these could explain how I was feeling. Google would throw out other suggestions. Multiple sclerosis kept popping up, and I was alarmed that my symptoms seemed to fit. *My goodness, could it really be that serious?* I wondered.

I took the last two weeks of work prior to the Christmas break as easily as I could. I did everything I needed to do and performed all my duties, but I held back a little and avoided getting involved in anything new. My symptoms continued to worsen, especially the dizziness. When I walked down the street, I found it difficult to stay in a straight line, and I was worried that it might look like I had been drinking. It would feel like someone was trying to push me over from the side. It would start on my right side, then it would suddenly switch to my left, and a few steps later it would change again and feel like someone was pushing me from the front.

Buddhist practice helped me cope with these symptoms. The momentum of that daily sitting carried me to my Zendo even when I didn't feel like it. For the first time in my life, the thoughts swirling through my mind as I sat in meditation all related to my health. *What could be wrong with me? Could it be a brain tumor? Could it be MS? Will I die or be unable to work again? Am I scared of dying?*

I recalled a story about an American woman that has always stuck in my mind. She was sick and scared after receiving a cancer diagnosis, and she only had a few years left to live. She traveled the world, looking for treatments and answers from doctors and spiritual teachers. But it took a meeting with a Tibetan Buddhist monk to really bring her back to herself. She traveled to India and attended a talk by the monk, and at the end of his lecture she told him, "I don't know what to do with myself or my life because I'm dying." To her surprise, the monk paused and then began to laugh before saying, with a beaming smile,

"We are all dying." This was enough to help the woman see that all she had to do was be present to her life and live well, whatever the circumstances.

All things are impermanent and eventually pass. This maybe sounds dramatic on one level, but it is true. Our lives are short, so I wanted to live mine well and free of fear. I had always been inspired by old Buddhist paintings from China and Japan depicting beautiful mountain landscapes. Often, if you look closely at these paintings, you will find someone sitting in meditation—a tiny speck in a hut— or walking on a remote mountain. These paintings said it all to me. Human life is beautiful, but in the scheme of the cosmos, our lives are tiny and insignificant. Our job is to play our part well and join the great dance of life, living peacefully and at one with "the way." When the time comes to let go, there is no need for fear.

Now that the kids were adults, Christmas was not quite so hectic, and I looked forward to my two-week break and getting some rest. My hope was that these symptoms would disappear of their own accord. Beth and I had a night away planned on the 28 December, and we stayed at one of our favorite hotels, Malmaison in Dundee. We checked into the hotel and fell asleep on the bed when we arrived. Our jobs had exhausted both of us.

The room had a lovely roll-top tub, and we both enjoyed a bath once we woke up. Later we ate a beautifully prepared three-course meal in the hotel restaurant, afterwards heading down to the bar to have a cocktail or two, piña coladas for me and mojitos for Beth. We had a lovely evening and didn't talk about my health at all. We discussed what was going on in the world, how the kids were progressing in life, and we had fun joking and reminiscing about the past and discussing our hopes for the future. It was great after all these years to still enjoy each other's company and feel so in love.

The next morning, we went down for breakfast and got a seat by the window. The Malmaison is close to the Tay estuary, and the window looked onto the Victoria and Albert museum with the Tay estuary's waters flowing seawards behind it. I couldn't keep my eyes off the beautiful view as I sat and ate my breakfast. After breakfast we enjoyed another relaxing bath and slept in each other's arms for an hour or so. We had to check out at noon, so we packed our bags and were soon ready to go. I sat on the edge of the bed and put on my shoes. Beth asked how I was feeling. It dawned on me that I felt almost symptom-free. Perhaps the doctor was right and all I needed was a good rest.

We left the hotel feeling relaxed, content, and deeply in love. It was a perfect moment. Relieved that I had managed to enjoy our night away, for the first time in a few weeks I felt content, at ease, and well. We drove to nearby Broughty Ferry, a beautiful, old, traditional part of Dundee, right on the banks of the Tay estuary. We parked the car and took a walk along the waterfront, passing the old fishermen's houses and the many quaint taverns, cafés, and restaurants. We visited Broughty Ferry castle and enjoyed walking through the rooms of the old building.

Beth and I love Scottish history, and we visit castles and places of historic significance whenever we have the chance. As I climbed the steep stairs, the weakness in my legs and the dizziness returned. Initially I did not say anything to Beth; I knew that she would be worried about me, and we were having such a great time that I didn't want it to be spoiled. As we left the castle to go and get a coffee and a bite to eat, I felt like a different person from the one who had entered the castle only an hour ago. My legs felt weak, my head was spinning, and my hands and feet were numb and tingling. I felt deeply disappointed.

We sat in a café on Broughty Ferry high street and ordered coffee and scones with butter and jam. As we sat speaking, I felt the life slowly draining from me and found it hard to fully concentrate on what Beth was saying. I could not help wondering what the hell was going on with me. I did not need to say anything to Beth; she just knew I was not right.

"Hamish, has it come back? You look tired."

"Beth, I can't believe it. I feel terrible. It started when we were in the castle, and it seems to be getting worse."

I saw the worry on Beth's face. We were due to visit her sister, Heather, and her husband, Gordon, at their home in Arbroath just a few miles along the coast. "Do you still want to go?" Beth asked. I felt terrible, but I didn't want to let her down as she loved visiting her sister, so we made the visit.

Heather and Gordon always gave us a great welcome, and I knew I would be okay in their hands. During the visit I sat on their sofa, and it felt like I was being sucked into it by a giant hoover that was also sucking every piece of energy out of me. I got through the visit, but I felt so weak and dizzy that I never moved from that seat.

This came as a shock. What was going on with me? I did everything I could during my two-week holiday to relax, but the symptoms persisted and if anything had gotten worse. When I returned to work in the new year, I felt the same. I managed to get through the first few days, and I wanted to keep going—until I saw my doctor at the end of the week.

On the day of my appointment, I felt worse than ever. The dizziness felt more permanent now, as did the weakness in my legs, hands, and feet. My shoulder and hip were extremely sore, and I felt fatigued. The doctor called me into her room and asked how I was. I'd made a double appointment (thirty minutes) as I had a lot to tell her. I explained my symptoms and how I had relaxed over the festive holiday, but my symptoms remained and had worsened.

She listened to my every word, watching me very closely as I spoke. When I finished, she looked me in the eye and said, "Do you know what I think is wrong with you, Hamish? You're stressed."

She continued, "Everything about you oozes stress, Hamish. The way you hold yourself, the way you speak. I see a lot of patients in my surgery who are stressed, so I have a lot of experience in this."

Dr. Simpson went on, "The symptoms you're experiencing could all be related to stress. In fact, I would say I am 98 percent confident that your symptoms are related to stress. All your blood tests came back fine. I'll tell you what I'm proposing we do for you. I'm going to refer you to neurology, just in case, just to be sure it's not something else, but as I say, I'm sure it's not something more sinister. Are you worried it could be something else?"

"Yes, I've been reading up about my symptoms and what could be causing them. I'm worried it could be MS."

The doctor said that my symptoms didn't match that illness. "I think we need to get you out of the work situation for a while, though."

These words struck me like a train. *Get me out of my work situation! How? I'm the CEO; I can't just take time off!* I was dumbfounded by what was happening and what the doctor was saying. She seemed to realize that this came as a shock to me.

"What I'm going to suggest is that you go home and have a think about me signing you off sick from work. You need to get out of there for a while and let us see if your symptoms improve. Meanwhile, I'm going to make a referral to neurology so we can be sure there's not something else at play. Also, I am going to prescribe you a course of citalopram, which is an antidepressant."

The word *antidepressant* felt like another shock. "Why on earth would I need an antidepressant? I don't feel depressed in the slightest," I said, exasperated.

To her credit, the doctor remained perfectly calm. "Hamish, I don't think that you're depressed, but there is evidence that taking a mild antidepressant, even when a patient does not feel depressed, can reduce the symptoms you're experiencing."

This answer made me feel slightly better, but my mind was reeling. I took the prescription reluctantly and agreed that I would think about getting signed off and would call her once I'd thought all this information through.

I got into the car and considered what to do. My first thought was to go to work and just get on with things and then use the weekend to consider what the doctor had said. I started to drive. But I did not feel myself. The conversation with the doctor had shaken me to my core. As I drove, I mused.

Maybe I should go home just for a cup of coffee, relax and meditate for thirty minutes, and ground myself before I go into work. Yes, that's what I'll do. I turned the car and headed home. When I got back to the house, I made myself a coffee and sat in my living room.

Being a CEO is stressful. On one level, I recognized that I carry a lot of stress—always thinking about the company, our finances, how our services are performing. As a CEO I'm always on show, chairing meetings, speaking to the media and politicians and other senior people across the north of Scotland. I am very engaged with staff and make myself available to them and participate in meetings as often as I can.

On reflection there was no doubt I have had to deal with a lot of difficult situations over the last seven years. Steven and Elaine sprang to mind, along with the constant worry about the company's finances and my frustrations with the board. Had all these things scarred me deeply until my mind just couldn't take any more?

Surely not, said another voice in my mind. Although these aspects of my job are all stressful, I always felt that I was dealing with the stress. *When people get stressed, they start to lose control, clearly showing signs of their stress and anxiety. They're quick to anger, lack clarity, have confusion and doubt. Aren't they?* I didn't feel like this. *Also, I'm a Buddhist. Buddhists are calm and serene and cope with the world. Don't they?* I sipped my coffee, my mind racing, and felt about as far from peace and serenity as I'd experienced in many a year.

I looked at my work diary on my phone, and there was nothing in it that day. It would do no harm not to go in. To keep things right, I sent a text to Norman asking for a day's annual leave, and he quickly replied, "No problem."

My body was agitated and full of tension. It dawned on me that perhaps I had not been as calm and peaceful as I liked to think I was for some time now. I poured myself a bath with Epsom salts. It felt glorious to melt into the waters. Dr. Simpson's words played in my mind time and time again.

Meditation teaches to be patient and to ground yourself on a level below the organ we call the brain. As my mind raced, I was aware of that peace, that connectedness which is beyond words, holding me in its space, even in this moment that had clearly shaken me. There is something bigger than me, than you, than us all. It doesn't matter what you call it—God, Buddha, Allah. Just experience it. It's closer than you think.

After my bath I dressed in loose, comfortable clothing and made my way to the Zendo. I offered incense to the Buddha and dedicated it to all beings in the world who, like me, were experiencing inner turmoil that day. *You are not alone*, I thought. *I feel the same way*. I bowed and took my place on the meditation stool as the Buddha sat watching. Incense smoke filled all corners of the room and wafted down the hall, permeating the house with its lovely teaching and smell. Could my practice likewise permeate me with wisdom?

I set the meditation timer for thirty minutes, rang my bell three times, and bowed to begin. I settled my breath and sat upright, giving myself to this moment. To my surprise, I felt a deep peace. Even in the midst of this mental turmoil, I found some respite—a sense of compassion for myself and how lost I felt at that moment, and again a deep empathy and connection with the many other beings out there. I sensed the turmoil and suffering in my own life but also across the whole globe. A deep unease.

This feeling was profound, but it did not scare me. It did not depress me. Instead I felt a deep sense of how important the Buddhist precepts are. Living with compassion suddenly felt so important. We are all frail and vulnerable at times. The person who was rude in the street, the person tooting their car horn at me, the person who turned away—what is their backstory, their pain, their suffering? The ancients told us to expect nothing and never judge. We are all human and deserving of compassion.

I sat in a deep and profound peace for ten minutes or more. Then the dam of thoughts broke and flowed through my mind. I still felt grounded in one sense, but my mind now filled with the doctor's words and my fears. Had I just been kidding myself? Had I been trying to follow the Buddhist way but was so caught up in the role of CEO that I'd built a huge idea of "self," ideas built on "me" as the all-conquering CEO, impervious to troubles and able to cope with all life throws at me?

Had I built an idea of self around what a Buddhist should be? Calm, serene, and reflective, compassionate to all I meet. Had I forgotten to be compassionate to myself? Surely Buddhism points to something deeper than just being "nice"? I felt it was time to contemplate these issues, but it would take a while to break down these walls of self that I had erected around myself. But somehow I knew this was the start of a new journey, and the walls were waiting to be dismantled. The first cracks had begun to appear, perhaps a long time ago, although I hadn't paid attention to them.

I spent the rest of the day relaxing. I meditated again and tidied up the house and took a short walk and enjoyed mindfully listening to the sounds of the birds and the wind in the trees. Beth arrived home from work, and we sat and had tea. She listened to me as I told her about what the doctor had said and how shocked I felt.

I finished speaking, and Beth spoke after a long pause. I could tell she was concerned for me and thinking seriously about her response. "Hamish, my love, I hope you know how much I love you and how deeply glad I am that I have you to share this life with. But I agree with your doctor, and I think you are very stressed. You rarely take time off work and never take time back. You seem to always be thinking about RCC, and I don't think you ever really let it go. You've developed nervous tics and twitches that weren't there before you became the CEO, but when I've tried to speak to you about how distant you've been and how stressed you appear, you always bat my concerns away.

"I've worried about these things, Hamish," she continued. "Yes, it's been great having more money as a family, but you and I both know that money is superficial and that the spiritual life is most important. Our health is far more important than money, and I just want my old Hamish back. You are grumpier than you ever were, and you are rigid in your approach to life. The carefree, fun-loving Hamish I married doesn't seem to be around much these days. But what worries me most, Hamish, and it tells me that you're not seeing clearly just now, is the fact you're only *thinking* about staying off work. For god's sake! You are constantly dizzy, parts of your body are numb and tingling, your shoulder and hip are sore, you are fatigued and feel weak, and you don't know if it is a good idea to be signed off work! Jesus, you're a mess, and you need to look after yourself, so please take time off your work and get better."

As Beth finished what felt like a devastating intervention and a call back to reality for me, tears flowed down her cheek. She came over to me and gave me the warmest and most loving cuddle I had ever experienced. We embraced for a long time. She then moved back and looked me in the eye. "Hamish, I love you, but I want you to call the doctor on Monday and get signed off. You need to remove yourself from work and focus on you for a change."

That conversation will live with me forever. Beth knew me better than anyone, and she had pulled away my veil. I knew she was right. I phoned the doctor on Monday, and she signed me off for a month.

Monday 12 January 2020 was the first time a doctor had signed me off from work in quite a long time. Several years back I'd had the flu for two weeks, but that had been it, in all my working days. This all felt very strange, but Beth had helped me see that it had to be done. *What will I do with my time?* I wondered. I felt the first thing to do was to ground myself and focus on my Buddhist practice.

At the beginning of my time off, I tried to have three or four meditation periods a day. My mind was agitated and my body full of tension. I still had to force myself to the Zendo and to work at my practice and remain mindful as I went about my life. My body was physically tight, and Beth said I looked stiff and sore. She suggested I try alternative therapies and yoga to help me. I contemplated this in meditation, and my first reaction was to shudder and say, *No, this is not for me.*

Why had my guard gone up when the woman I love made a loving and helpful suggestion? The more I thought about my reaction, the more appalled I became. At one time I would have embraced these suggestions and given them a try. What did I have to lose?

After only a few days of stilling my mind it became clear to me that Beth was right: I had become rigid in my thinking and less carefree. *Why?* I wondered. I did not have the answers yet, but they slowly began to appear. I had become consumed with the CEO role. Each big decision had slowly chipped away at me. The burden I carried had seeped into my soul, muscles, joints, and mind. I had forgotten life's small pleasures. I used to stop and look at a beautiful sunset and go out bird-watching with my dad every week; I kept fit, and my family and friends would have said that I was fun-loving and mellow. These things had all started to disappear.

On reflection, I could see that the job took so much out of me sometimes that when I got home in the evening or the weekend came around, I just did not have the energy or enthusiasm to do fun things. I couldn't "see" Beth and the kids. I'd been isolating myself for a long time.

Over the next month, I threw myself into reconnecting with Buddhism, my family, and life in general. I took Beth's advice and tried new things. Beth suggested yoga and shiatsu, so I gave them a try. She recommended a yoga class that ran out of Robert Gordon University's sport club. She'd attended before and thought it would be a nice, gentle introduction for me.

I was nervous when she took me along for the first time as I felt so weak and fatigued and my shoulder and hip felt very sore. To my surprise, despite my movement being seriously restricted because of my buckled body, I really enjoyed it. The class instructor, Roy, was inspirational. He was about sixty and open about the fact that he suffered from Parkinson's disease. Although this is classed as a major health condition, here he was, leading the class and bending himself into all sorts of fantastic stretches. Maybe, despite my health issues, I too could use yoga to improve my condition. There were some positions that I felt I could not get into, but that was okay.

What really hooked me was how I felt after the class. My body and mind felt relaxed, and I was not quite as stiff. I started doing yoga every day despite my fatigue and weakness. Slowly my body came back to me. It felt like the emotional wounds inflicted by challenging situations and characters like Steven and Elaine had been held in my body. But with yoga and meditation, they were being released.

For shiatsu, there was a well-known guy called Simon in Aberdeen's complementary health scene who had a good reputation, so I went to see him. We clicked straightaway, and I gained a lot of knowledge from him. Simon is a shiatsu practitioner, a Chinese herbalist, and yoga teacher.

I always want to understand the theory behind treatments I receive, and shiatsu, like acupuncture, works on the meridians in the body. Simon introduced me to the idea that meridians can get blocked through not living well and that stress, poor diet, negative mental attitude, and lack of exercise can all lead to these blocks. In Shiatsu, the practitioner uses their fingers to press down on and manipulate the meridian pressure points. By doing so they can detect blockages in Qi energy and help to clear the blockage.

It's safe to say that Simon and shiatsu had a profound effect on me. As a result of his shiatsu, I began to feel better, ever so slowly. But he also inspired me to read into diet and how it affects our body and mind. I had always presumed I had a good diet, but apparently I was just kidding myself.

Like most Buddhists, I was vegetarian, and I ate some fruit and vegetables every day. I ate rice and pasta and bread, but very little of it was wholemeal. Simon introduced me to the idea of eating more high-quality organic wholefoods and suggested introducing more legumes, beans, and grains into my diet. He also advised me to stop drinking so much coffee. This was a tough one, but I knew that I drank far too much of it. I gave it up completely and replaced it with herbal teas.

I started to feel better in myself, but progress was painfully slow. After my first month off, I was making improvements but still a long way from being well. The dizziness was still there, and I felt fatigued, my legs felt weak, and certain parts of my body felt numb. Although most of my symptoms were not quite as intense and had improved slightly, the doctor said I needed another month off at least. This did not come as such a shock this time, and I felt that psychologically this was progress. I had accepted that I was ill, and that stress could be a factor. I just wanted to get better now.

I kept progressing over the next few weeks until something strange happened. It was late morning, and I was sitting on my own, watching TV, when suddenly I felt sick. My stomach was churning, and it came on suddenly and unexpectedly. I moved off the sofa and lay on the floor to see if that made any difference. It did not help, so I stood and turned off the TV.

As I stood gazing out of my living room window, I knew something was not right. I felt strange; the world seemed strange. Colors and sounds seemed different. It was like an acid trip. I could tell that I was not thinking straight. I decided to go upstairs and lie down to see if this would pass. After climbing a few stairs, I immediately felt dizzy and worried I would fall. Despite not thinking clearly, I knew the danger of falling backwards down the stairs, so I threw myself forward and slowly clambered up on all fours. I got to the top of the stairs and slowly turned the corner on my hands and knees. Once I was round the corner, I held on to the banister and pulled myself to my feet. If I fell here, I would be okay.

I managed to walk to my bedroom where I lay down on my bed. I took a few deep breaths and drew upon my Buddhist training. These deep breaths allowed me to calm down a little and assess what was happening to me. *Am I having a stroke?* I wondered. I knew a simple test I could perform to indicate whether I was having a stoke. I raised my hands and arms above my head. I looked in the mirror and smiled, and then I stuck out my tongue and moved it to the right and left, relieved that I was able to perform these tasks.

But reality still felt different. In my confusion I can remember thinking, *Am I imagining this?* I decided to stand up and test how the world looked and felt from a standing position again. It only took a few seconds of standing for me to realize that I was not imagining this. I also had a strange feeling of euphoria. Despite these awful physical sensations, I felt elated, which, looking back on this incident, seems like a bizarre reaction.

I had the sense to realize it was dangerous for me to be alone. Would these symptoms get worse? My first thought was to phone Beth, and I sent her a text asking her to call me ASAP. Just after I sent the text, I heard her phone *ting* at the side of our bed.

I shouted a curse. Of all the days for her to forget her phone. This threw me slightly, and I took some more deep breaths to settle myself. Who to phone now? Most people I knew were at work. I did not want to panic my boys, so I called my dad. He realized immediately that something was up. Later he told me that my speech was slower than normal and slightly slurred. His first concern was that I was having a stroke. He got to my house quickly.

By this time, I felt slightly better and was keen to get up and go downstairs. I got off the bed myself, and my dad walked in front of me as we descended the stairs. The dizziness was still there, and I was nervous I would fall, but I made it down without incident. I glanced at my Buddhist altar and was reassured by the peaceful image of the Buddha silently watching me. He seemed to say, "Stay grounded. All things are impermanent, including this." If I had felt stronger, I would have bowed.

My dad and I spoke when we got to my living room, but my memory of what we talked about is unclear now. Then my phone rang, and it was Beth. I answered the phone by saying, "Beth, how can you call me? Your phone is upstairs. It's okay, my dad is here now."

"Hamish, what on earth are you saying, and why is your dad there?" she asked.

"I tried to text you and I heard your phone 'ting' at the side of our bed, so I asked my dad to come out and sit with me." Later Beth told me that when she called, I was making no sense at all, and she thought my speech sounded slurred. She asked me to put my dad on the phone, which I did, and he agreed to take me to A&E.

My dad dropped me at the door of the hospital and briefly spoke to Beth, who had made her way there. Eventually I was seen by an A&E doctor, who conducted a series of tests. She told me that she wanted me to see a neurologist and they would come and see me shortly.

After thirty minutes or so, a neurologist, Dr. McCarthy, came down to conduct further tests. I explained to her all that had been happening to me regarding my health over the last few months. She asked me what I thought was wrong with me and if I was worried it might be something in particular. I told her I was worried that my symptoms were similar to MS or a brain tumor. Dr. McCarthy reassured me that she did not think that I had either of these conditions. She explained that I would have reacted differently to the tests she had just performed.

Dr. McCarthy then asked me if I had ever come across the term *FND*. I had not heard, but she said that she was fairly sure this was what was happening to me. "FND stands for 'functional neurological disorder,' and it is a phenomenon that is not yet fully understood, although neurologists know that it's real and are able to identify it in people as a distinct neurological condition."

The doctor continued, "FND means that for some reason the signals that your body receives from your brain and the signals that come back to the brain are confused. This explains the dizziness and strange sensations across your body. I am not diagnosing you with FND just yet, as we need to get the MRI results first and then do some other investigations, but I think there is a strong likelihood that this is what is wrong with you. Do you have any questions, Hamish?"

"Yes, I do. My own GP seems to be adamant that my symptoms are caused by stress at work. Can FND be brought about by stress in someone's life?"

"Not necessarily, Hamish. Your GP is right that FND can be caused by stress in some people, and we now believe that people fall into three categories. The first category is those whose FND is brought on by stress. The second category are those whose FND is brought about by a traumatic event in their life, like an accident, abuse, a bereavement, or surgery. But we also have enough evidence to show clearly that there is a third category of people who develop FND where there seems to be no obvious trigger. Can I suggest that you Google 'Professor Jon Stone functional neurological disorder'? He is the leading authority on FND, and he has created a helpful website for people who have been diagnosed with this condition. It details the causes and how to deal with the symptoms and how to approach treatment. Read that, and we will see you again at the clinic to review your MRI scan." I thanked her for the advice and help, and off she went.

It had been quite a day, but there had been positives, and seeing a neurologist was helpful. I now had some indication about what might be wrong with me. I had never heard of FND, but I was certainly going to take Dr. McCarthy's advice.

Over the next few weeks, I rested as much as I could. I did my yoga once a day and meditated two to four times a day. When I did not feel weak, I went for short walks. I read Jon Stone's website, which was very comprehensive, telling me everything I needed to know about FND. Some of it was unsettling as it laid bare the difficulties some people can have—scary things like blackouts and difficulty with speech and mobility. Some people recover fully from FND, others recover to some degree, and others live with it for the rest of their lives.

The website made it clear that FND is caused by stress for some people. *Is it really stress that has done this to me? Could I really have been so oblivious to how it was affecting me?* This still seemed incredible, but I was beginning to think it might be true.

This was hard to accept from a CEO and Buddhist point of view. This revelation dented my CEO pride. I did not see myself as someone who was greatly affected by pressure. Sometimes I thrived on it. Through all the difficult situations I had dealt with, I never recognized that I was stressed. But here I was being told by yet another doctor that I had serious health symptoms likely caused by stress.

Over the coming weeks, as I meditated, my mind became more still and at peace each day. The more still my mind became, the more I realized how troubled my mind had been in the months leading up to becoming unwell. My mind had built a strong sense of how I should behave as a CEO and as a Buddhist. Unhelpfully, I had constructed a huge edifice of self around both aspects. Only now, with the aid of a long period off work, which allowed me to meditate deeply over weeks, did this become clear to me. This idea of who I was as a CEO and Buddhist was characterized by a strong belief that I should cope with stress.

However, I was human after all. I could see clearly now that the daily hassles, the major staffing issues, the perceived constant pressure and criticism from the board, and constantly operating within very tight financial margins had all taken their toll, even though I had not noticed it along the way. Each one left a mark deep in my soul and psyche. I did not think they were affecting me, but their negativity slowly built up within me until my mind and body could not keep up anymore. It was clear that my body and mind had gone haywire into what the doctors now call a functional neurological disorder.

What was important was to live now. Accept where I was in my Buddhist practice, my career, my health, and life. Let go of judgments;

I am where I am. I had the gift of seeing clearly again and knew it was time to let these ideas of who and what I should be fall away. They had played their part in my becoming ill.

As I sat meditating in my Zendo, feeling unwell and knowing it was time to let a lot of old beliefs fall apart, I felt oddly calm. Any fear I had about what the future held for me, including whether I could ever work again, dissipated. I felt something I had not felt strongly for some time. I felt optimistic about my future, whatever it might hold. Some of the words from the famous Zen poem called "The Excellent Mirror of Samadhi," written by Tozan Ryokai about 900 years ago, came to mind. In the poem he writes, "The sage will tell a trainee, who is feeling he is low and all inferior, that on his head there gleams a jeweled diadem, and on his body rich robes hang, and at his feet there is a footrest." As things started to fall apart, I could feel the diadem, rich robes, and footrest. Strangely, I felt glad to be alive.

CHAPTER 10

Where to Now?

> As you walk, eat and travel,
>
> Be where you are.
>
> Otherwise you will miss most of your life,
>
> —*The Buddha*

Where am I now? Where am I heading? What have I learned from my CEO experience? Can I be well enough to continue as a CEO? What about Buddhism and me? Where is my life heading now? These questions became prominent in my meditations. Had being a CEO made me ill? Had any of it been worth it?

I have been the CEO for more than seven years now. I remember the excitement I felt when I was first offered the post. I felt proud and set about trying to rectify problems that had held RCC back for years. Reflecting on those days, it probably was stressful from day one, but I felt that I had a supportive board and, during the first few years, a supportive leadership team. Although I had held other senior management posts, I had never been that person who is ultimately in charge of everything. It can be a scary place to be, but it can also feel exhilarating when you see positive changes begin to happen.

I remember how excited I felt at the end of my first full financial year in charge when we posted a surplus of £20,000. It might not seem like a lot, but when you consider RCC had made losses of more than £100,000 a year for the previous two years, it was a great achievement. We also started to improve our services, which in turn boosted staff morale. We sorted out our internal processes and support functions, such as IT, finance, administration, and HR, and as they improved, it helped our services function better and further boosted staff morale because the supports actually made their jobs easier instead of getting in their way. We also set ourselves goals, like creating a world-class staff culture and getting into the *Sunday Times* Top 100 companies to work for in the UK. We made it into the Top 100 every year I was in charge. I could not help but be proud of these achievements, and my confidence began to soar.

Buddhism cautions against pride and being full of your own self-importance. I tried not to get too caught up in ideas of how well I was doing. Did I manage this? I stuck with my meditation and Buddhist practice throughout these times. But my practice changed. I found it harder to stay grounded and live in the moment. I recognize that I rarely put RCC down. Even though I was good at leaving the office at 5:30, I would think about the company as I drove home, when I had my tea, and even when I meditated. Normally I would have been disappointed by this, but the excitement of what I was driving forward at RCC, and the changes I saw happening, took over and drove me on.

The real excitement was in the difference I was making to the people who needed RCC's services. I would have loved nothing more than to work directly with our customers and help support them in their time of need. But as a CEO, I was far removed from the frontline, and my contribution was different. When I took over the role, our main services worked with about 1,500 people per year. After seven years, we were now working with 4,000 people per year. It gave me immense satisfaction to help so many more people. These people would never know who I was and would never meet me. But I knew I had helped them.

Our customers and their families also told us that they valued our services and support and that we helped them greatly. I felt it was Buddhism in action. It was important for me to use the CEO role to extol the Buddhist principles that I believed in. It is my hope that I did this well. I treated staff well. I listened to their concerns, tried to fix things for them, created a workplace culture where they were treated well, but at the same time, we expected them to work hard and do a great job for our customers. This was the exciting part of the job.

Nobody connected with RCC would argue that I have not made significant changes. A lot has been written about the importance of values and compassion in leadership and within organizations. Although I seldom talked about Buddhism to my colleagues or board members, its teachings guided my leadership journey and guided me well, ensuring that I kept sound morals at the heart of everything I did. Trying to live by these values and apply them in my leadership role has shown me that treating staff well and encouraging them does produce great results.

Staff engagement is far from easy, and it takes up time, but it is worth it. I saw demotivated staff become great members of the team once we started to engage with them and they felt we were listening to their concerns. Once things started to change for the better, they felt it and began to enjoy coming to work. It was then easier to get them to buy into the idea of a high-performing culture where all staff sought to be and do their best. They began to take a pride in RCC and took pleasure in seeing us succeed.

Although most staff bought into the new culture, not everyone did. In fact, by far the biggest challenge I faced as a CEO, and as a Buddhist, was with people. I gained enormous benefit from sharing my leadership experiences with the fellowship of the CEOs. It struck me at these meetings that they all felt their biggest challenge, other than their board, was staff. No matter what I did, there were always members of staff who could only see the negative.

I am grateful for being a CEO. It has shown me things that I might never have seen. It has shown me that most people do pull together and try to do their best. Most people do come into work with the intention of doing a good job. But it also showed me a darker side of the human spirit. I have described some of these darker incidents in this book, but there were many others. It left me deeply saddened to witness the levels people will go to prove a point or score a victory.

I have heard the argument for compulsory military service, positing the idea that two years in the military would teach people responsibility and how to live well. I don't necessarily agree with this, but I have come to wonder if everyone should be made to be a manager for two years. It would show people just how complex every situation is. It would show that the people dynamics in their team or department are far more intricate than they ever imagined. It would maybe show that colleagues they thought were good members of the team were not as they seemed. From a manager's perspective, some staff might not be so good after all. In short, the experience would show how hard being a leader really is and it may bring about more compassion in the workplace.

What did I learn from these negative experiences? The first thing I learned is that you need to deal with them head-on. If someone is undermining your leadership, you must let them know that you're not going to tolerate the situation. Then let them know the types of behavioral changes you expect to see moving forward and what the consequences will be if they do not change.

On a personal level, I found these conversations hard. But I never avoided them. In my career, I observed that the most damaging thing to any organization, team, or department's performance was not dealing with toxic staff. I have seen managers, sometimes very senior managers, ignore the damage rogue members of staff have caused across teams. This often had devastating effects on productivity levels and morale and stopped these teams from achieving something great. It certainly stopped many of them from delivering fantastic services to their customers.

Why do leaders shy away from these situations? I can only presume it's because it seems easier to ignore it. To shut their office door and just let the staff team deal with it. Many managers have never been mentored by senior staff on how to tackle these situations and feel scared to open difficult conversations. I vowed when I became CEO that this would never happen on my watch.

Where does Buddhism fit into this? I always believe in giving people a chance to rectify their behaviors. Quite often, people genuinely have not appreciated the impact their behavior is having on their team. Once it is pointed out to them, they often change quickly. Buddhism informed how I approached these meetings. I hope that the staff member would say after such a meeting that I had been clear and direct about the problem but also respectful and supportive towards them. I would have highlighted their strengths and how, if they focused on these areas, they could make an even greater contribution to their team and the overall work of the company. Most people may have felt slightly embarrassed by these conversations, but they accepted what was said and made efforts to change, and we all moved on positively. I would encourage any leader to tackle these issues and never let them fester.

However, some people were in a different kind of bracket altogether. I cannot say for sure what motivates the Stevens and Elaines of this world. Perhaps they were resentful of the changes I brought about. They both seemed to have a destructive element to their personalities, which makes me think that a lot of their behaviors were rooted in their psyche; maybe they did not fully know why they acted as they did.

My job was not to be their psychologist but to ensure that everyone in the company was pulling together and heading in the same direction. Dealing with both situations was unpleasant, and at times I felt very lonely, especially when I felt my whole leadership team was against me. But on reflection, I'm so glad that I dealt with these situations despite it being a lot of hard work, physically and mentally.

I have no doubt that the Stevens and Elaines of this world always believe that the company will fall apart without them. In my experience, the exact opposite happens. Someone eager and ambitious to move on in their career steps into these roles and usually far exceeds what the previous negative post holder had achieved. Although I went through a lot of pain to move these people on, I never once regretted it. It sent a clear message to the other staff in the company as well—that at the helm was a fair-minded and honest CEO who would encourage and support them every step of the way, but if they messed about and tried to be mischievous, he would not tolerate it for long. This was no bad thing. Buddhism is all about compassion and treating people well, but it does not say you cannot stand up for yourself, for what you feel is right.

Is being a Buddhist, or perhaps following any religion or spiritual practice, compatible with being a CEO? Early in my career, I often saw the boss as the bad guy and never associated being the bad guy with being a good Buddhist. Being the boss, I presumed, involved a lot of telling people off and being involved in negative things like disciplinaries and sacking people. Buddhist teaching and practice is often conducted in silence and involves meditation, living by the Buddhist precepts and living a quiet, peaceful life, and living as much as you can in the moment. Surely this is not compatible with being a CEO?

Even after seven years, I'm not sure of the answer to this question. There is no doubt that leadership and business in general could benefit from more Buddhist leaders. I sometimes look on the business world and feel ashamed when I read about good staff being discarded or the environment being degraded, all for profit. Leadership should be value driven, and Buddhist values are something to be proud of and should not be hidden from the world. I see no reason why Buddhists and Buddhist principles are not compatible with great leadership. If more companies or individual leaders approached their leadership role and developed a style that is compassionate and encouraging, I have no doubt that it would improve any company's performance as well as individual staff members' enjoyment of their job and their life.

However, personally, I found a continual tension between being a Buddhist practitioner and my role. In my mind there are at least two versions of me. One me dreams of living the contemplative life, a quiet, peaceful life, the hermit life. A life full of regular visits to Throssel for retreats with the monks and long walks with Beth in the hills. A life full of simple living, simple eating, meditation, contemplative walks, and lots of silence. This kind of lifestyle just seems to be the natural conclusion of a meditative life. The more I meditate and practice mindfulness, the more I naturally want to be silent and contemplative.

But then real life kicks in for many of us and takes us down a different route. The deep love I have for Beth and my children means I want to provide the best for them—provide them with the best house I can, take them on holidays, and do nice things as a family. Compromise my needs for their needs. This is just life, and I do not regret a minute of it.

Sitting here, reflecting on my life, I can see how I ended up being the boss. By living the Buddhist life, I tried to do my best in my employment and over time developed the expertise and skills that eventually led me on this crazy leadership journey. It has at times felt like a strange place for a Buddhist to be. It certainly hasn't been very peaceful, and the stresses of the job led to less peaceful times on my meditation mat. My family would tell you that I changed almost the moment I was promoted. It was subtle at first, and not dramatic. I've been a less fun Hamish and walk less and less with Beth. The job has consumed me, as I guess it would consume anyone. It would be hard for it not to. Even when I'm home or in the Zendo at Throssel, many of the thoughts that swirl through my mind are of budgets, service performance, or what I'm going to do about the endless challenges and difficult situations the company is experiencing. After seven years, I'm not sure that this is how I want to live this precious life.

It has certainly been one hell of a journey: a roller-coaster ride, from the highs of seeing the company thrive under my leadership to the low moments of witnessing the worst aspects of human behavior.

Being away from the office has enabled me to see and accept how unsettled I was in those moments when people turned against me. Still, I'm in awe of the opportunity that presented itself, ultimately enabling me to grow as a person, to see life raw and feel the thrill of overseeing it all as the CEO.

So, am I where I expected to be? No. At the age of only forty-nine, I'm still signed off sick from work with no certainty as to whether I'll ever recover. I didn't see this coming. I'm still working on all these questions with my doctor and neurologist, but my intuition tells me this has everything to do with the job. I still ask myself, *Why me?* Not every CEO becomes stressed to the point of developing a neurological disorder. I think some things come down to bad luck and even an individual's genetic inheritance.

But when we developed our fellowship of the CEOs, I had the benefit of becoming close personal friends with many other CEOs. I observed and learned from people who were dynamic, inspirational, great leaders and whose compassion had led them to the helm of a multitude of caring charities. I also observed the stress and ill health many of them were subject to due to the pressures of their job. This was a revelation to me. The idea that the CEO should be impervious to the stresses and strains of the workplace is a myth that needs debunking. Companies should take seriously the wellbeing of all their staff, including their CEO.

My own diagnosis has really made me stop and think. Any fanciful thoughts I had of the gladiator CEO, impervious to stress and struggle, have now fallen away. After all the highs and lows, I suddenly feel very human and very vulnerable, but also humble. Having FND makes my own impermanence seem very real. Buddhism teaches us to be wary of setting up ideas about ourselves, built on the need for success or striving to "be something." It teaches that every human has value, whether his or her job is held in high esteem in the eyes of the world or not. I see now we need to wear lightly the different identities we take on; they can change and be taken from us in the blink of an eye.

I have always been a great believer in my intuition, so what is it telling me now? It's time for a change of direction. Life comes and life goes, just like the tides. Now that the kids are older, maybe Beth and I could live a different kind of life, one that is contemplative and slower paced, like the days of old, like the sages of old. Maybe I should place my hands in gassho and bow to RCC for all it has taught me. Whatever the reason for my illness, RCC has played its part, and my gut tells me if I keep working this hard, my life will be short.

There is no concrete thing I can call "me," other than illusions I have built in my own mind. There is something deeper to connect with, and one day I will merge with it when I die. There is nothing to fear about that. It is "the way."

But it's not time to let go fully just yet. I feel there is more to come. A more peaceful life calls me. The way is not clear, but ideas are slowly forming. Maybe my dream of living a hermit's life will yet come to fruition and one day I will wonder off into the Assynt mountains and live like the sages of old. Perhaps that's a journey I can write about, too.

ACKNOWLEDGMENTS

I would like to thank a number of people who have assisted me with the production of my book. First of all, I would like to express my gratitude to Koehler Books for publishing my book. A special thanks goes to Greg Fields, the acquisitions editor at Koehler Books, for picking out my book from the many he receives. I also want to thank him for the assistance and advice he has given me along the way, all of which have made my book better. I would also like to thank John Koehler for all of his help.

I would like to thank my wife, Andrea, for being there for me through thick and thin and also for helping me to edit the first draft of the book. I thank my parents, Brian and Hilda Lawrie, and my sister-in-law, Aileen Hunter, for reading the first two drafts of the book and giving me detailed feedback. I also thank my brother, Euan Lawrie, and my niece and nephew, Jaime Boath and Jon Hunter, for reading an early draft and giving me very helpful feedback. A huge thank-you also to my good friends Bill and Lesley Keir, who both took time out of their busy schedules to read the first draft. All of your efforts are greatly appreciated.

Also a huge thanks to Reverend Master Leandra Robertshaw, abbot of Throssel Hole Buddhist Monastery, for supporting the book, and I would like to thank Reverend Master Favian Straughan, prior of Portobello Buddhist Priory, and Reverend Master Mugo White for reading the first draft and giving me feedback and support. I want you both to know that means a lot to me.

REFERENCES

Ozeki, Ruth. *A Tale for the Time Being*. Edinburgh: Canongate Books, 2013.

Lawrie, Brian, and Mick McKie. *Mountains and Rivers: Dee Valley Poems from Source to Sea*. Aberdeen: Malfranteaux Concepts, 2015.

Ryokan. *One Robe, One Bowl: The Zen Poetry of Ryokan*. Translated and introduced by John Stevens. Trumble, Conn.: Weatherhill, 1997.

Han-Shan. *Cold Mountain: 100 Poems by the T'ang poet Han-Shan*. Translated by Burton Watson. New York: Columbia University Press, 1970.

Roberts, Shinshu. *Being-Time: A Practitioner's Guide to Dogen's Shobogenzo Uji*. Somerville: Wisdom Publications, 2018.

Uchiyama, Kosho. *How To Cook Your Life*. Shambala Publication Inc, 2005.

Printed in the USA
CPSIA information can be obtained
at www.ICGtesting.com
LVHW050425280524
781480LV00003B/564